PROUD GREEK, RUTHLESS REVENGE
CHANTELLE SHAW

~ GREEK HUSBANDS ~

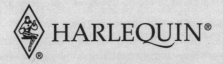

HARLEQUIN®

TORONTO • NEW YORK • LONDON
AMSTERDAM • PARIS • SYDNEY • HAMBURG
STOCKHOLM • ATHENS • TOKYO • MILAN • MADRID
PRAGUE • WARSAW • BUDAPEST • AUCKLAND

Recycling programs
for this product may
not exist in your area.

ISBN-13: 978-0-373-52756-4

PROUD GREEK, RUTHLESS REVENGE

First North American Publication 2010.

PROUD GREEK,
RUTHLESS REVENGE

In memory of my darling dad, Bob Gibbs, who encouraged me to write and was so proud of me.

CHAPTER ONE

'TAHLIA, you look divine.' Crispin Blythe, owner of the contemporary art gallery Blythe of Bayswater, greeted Tahlia Reynolds effusively. 'Those baubles you're wearing must be worth a small fortune.'

'A large fortune, actually,' Tahlia replied dryly, moving her hand to the ornate sapphire and diamond necklace at her throat. 'These "baubles" are top-grade Kashmiri sapphires.'

'Let me guess. A present from Daddy? Reynolds Gems' profits must be booming.' Crispin's smile faded slightly. 'It's good to know that some businesses are unaffected by this wretched recession.'

Tahlia frowned at the faintly bitter note in Crispin's voice. She had heard rumours that the gallery was suffering from the downturn in the economy, and for a moment she was tempted to reveal that things were far from rosy with her father's jewellery company, but she kept quiet. Reynolds Gems' financial problems would be public knowledge if the company went into liquidation, but they were not at that point yet. Perhaps she was being unrealistic, but she refused to give up hope that the company her father had built up over the past thirty years could be saved. It would not be for want of trying, she thought grimly. Her parents had used all their savings trying to keep

Reynolds afloat, while she had worked for no salary for the past three months, and had traded in the sports car her father had given her three years ago, for her twenty-first birthday, for a battered old Mini.

In desperation she had even sold her few items of jewellery, as well as many of the designer clothes that she had once been able to afford. The dress she was wearing tonight was on loan from a friend who owned a boutique, and the sapphire and diamond necklace was not her own—though it was one of Reynolds Gems' most valued pieces, stunningly beautiful and instantly eye-catching. Her father had asked her to wear it tonight in the hope of drumming up new business for Reynolds, but she was terrified of losing it, and knew she was going to spend the evening constantly checking that it was still around her neck.

She followed Crispin into the gallery, accepted a glass of champagne from a waiter, and glanced around at her fellow guests who were congregated in groups, admiring the paintings by the artist Rufus Hartman. Tahlia nodded to one or two acquaintances and allowed her eyes to drift. They came to an abrupt halt on the man who was standing on the other side of the room.

'Who is that?' she murmured curiously, feeling her heart jolt violently beneath her ribs. In a room packed with good-looking, successful men, the simmering virility of this particular man set him apart from the crowd.

'I assume you're referring to the Greek hunk in the Armani?' Crispin said archly, following the direction of her gaze. 'Thanos Savakis, billionaire head of Savakis Enterprises. He bought out the Blue-Sky holiday chain a couple of years ago, and owns several five-star hotels around the world. Careful, darling, you're drooling,' Crispin murmured wickedly as Tahlia continued to stare. 'A word of warning: Savakis has a reputation as a womaniser. His affairs are discreet, but numerous—and short-lived. Commitment is not a word associated with Thanos Savakis—unless it's his commitment to making even more money to add to his enviable fortune,' Crispin finished with a theatrical sigh.

'Workaholic womanisers are definitely not my type,' Tahlia murmured faintly, dragging her gaze from the man and taking a sip of champagne. But her eyes were drawn inexorably towards him, and she was glad that he was looking down at the dainty blonde who was hanging onto his arm because it gave her a chance to study him.

Tall and lean, with broad shoulders sheathed in an expertly tailored jacket, he was mesmerising, and Tahlia quickly realised that she was not the only woman in the room to be fascinated by him. With his classically sculpted features, bronzed skin and gleaming black hair, which was cropped short to emphasise the proud tilt of his head, he was stunningly handsome. But teamed with his blatant sex appeal Thanos Savakis possessed some indefinable quality—a magnetism and self-assurance that set him apart from other men. He would command any situation, Tahlia decided. She sensed his innate arrogance, and although he appeared to be giving his full attention to the pretty blonde at his side, she detected the giveaway signs that he was growing impatient of his companion's chatter.

The woman was a little too eager, Tahlia mused. Instinct told her that a man as self-possessed as Thanos Savakis would be irritated by any hint of neediness, and as she watched he carefully but firmly extricated himself from the blonde's grip and strolled into the adjoining gallery.

Gorgeous, but definitely out of her league, Tahlia decided, giving herself a mental shake as she slowly became aware once more of the babble of voices around her, and the clink of champagne flutes on a silver tray as a waiter walked past. She was shocked by the effect the sexy Greek had had on her—especially as the width of the room had separated them and he hadn't even glanced in her direction. She could not remember ever being so aware of a man. Not even James.

Her mouth tightened. Six months ago her relationship with James Hamilton had come to a shocking and explosive end, and since then she had struggled to piece her shattered heart back together. But the bitterness she felt towards him still burned as corrosively as on the night she had discovered his treachery.

'Tahlia, darling, that's vintage Krug you're gulping down, not fizzy water.' Crispin's laconic drawl dragged Tahlia back to the present. 'Can I get you another?'

She grimaced as she glanced down and saw that she had drained her glass without realising it. 'No, thanks. I'd better not.'

Crispin gave her an impatient look. 'Oh, live daringly for once. A few glasses of bubbly will help you relax.'

'Correction, a few glasses will have me giggling inanely,' Tahlia said dismally. 'And, after the recent press stories about me, I really could do without being snapped by the paparazzi clearly the worse for drink.'

Crispin gave her an amused glance. 'Yes, the tabloids do seem to have excelled themselves,' he agreed. 'The headline "Gems girl Tahlia Reynolds blamed for marriage break-up of TV soapstar Damian Casson" was particularly attention-grabbing.'

Tahlia flushed. 'It isn't true,' she said tensely. 'I was set up. I've only ever met Damian once, when we were guests at a book launch party held at a hotel. He was knocking back champagne all night and kept pestering me. I told him to get lost. The next morning he came over to my table at breakfast to apologise. We got chatting, and he told me he'd got drunk the previous night after he'd rowed with his wife and she had refused to go to the party with him. When I left, he offered to carry my bag to the car—hence the picture of the two of us emerging from the hotel together. Neither of us had expected the media to be hanging around at nine o'clock on a Sunday morning—or at least,' she said slowly, 'I hadn't expected them to be there.'

Anger formed a tight knot in Tahlia's chest at the realisation that Damian had undoubtedly been aware of the presence of the media.

'I was shocked when a journalist asked about our relationship, but Damian told me to leave it to him and he would explain that we were simply friends.'

Instead, the handsome young actor had told the press a pack of lies about their 'amazing night of sizzling sex', Tahlia thought bitterly. If Damian's intention had been to make his wife jealous, it had obviously worked. Beverly Casson had been quoted saying she was 'distraught' that 'party girl' Tahlia had stolen her man. The story had been a scoop for the journalists—the sort of thing that would boost sales of the tabloid, and no one seemed to care that it was untrue, or that Tahlia's reputation was now in tatters.

'This sort of adverse publicity is one of the drawbacks of allowing myself to be in the public eye,' she said dully. 'For months the press have made me out to be a vacuous bimbo who turns up to every event—even the opening of an envelope. It's the price I've had to pay for promoting Reynolds Gems.'

Tahlia bit her lip. When she had graduated from university three years ago her father had made her a partner of his company and given her the role of PR executive. But the global recession had hit Reynolds hard, and in an attempt to raise the company's profile she had reluctantly agreed to feature in an advertising campaign. She had then appeared in glossy magazines, attended numerous social events, modelling fabulous diamonds and precious gems from the Reynolds Gems collection.

Before she had left for the gallery tonight she had learned that all her hard work had been for nothing.

Peter Reynolds had looked grave as he'd explained that, despite the campaign, profits at all three of Reynolds Gems' jewellery shops were down. 'To be frank, Tahlia, Reynolds is facing bankruptcy,' he'd told her. 'I've approached every major bank and financial institution for help, but they've all refused to lend us any more money.' Tahlia's heart had ached when her father had dropped his head into his hands in a gesture of utter despair. 'I'm at rock bottom,' he'd admitted hoarsely. 'I've no more money left to stave off our creditors. The only glimmer of hope on the horizon is an equity firm, Vantage Investments, who have expressed an interest in buying out the company. I've arranged to meet their CEO next week.'

Tahlia could not forget the lines of strain of her father's face, but she forced her mind back to the present and glanced around the gallery, aware that fretting about Reynolds' financial situation was not going to help. She had dreaded the prospect of attending the exhibition tonight, when her supposed love-life was headline news, but Rufus Hartman was a close friend from her university days and she could not have missed his first major exhibition.

As she strolled around the gallery with Crispin she was conscious of the curious stares from some of the other guests. 'I wonder how many people here tonight think I'm a heartless marriage-breaker,' she muttered bitterly.

'No one believes a word that's written in the gutter press,' Crispin assured her breezily.

Tahlia wished she shared his confidence, but for a moment she was tempted to slink into a quiet corner and remain there for the rest of the night. But that was ridiculous; she had done nothing to be ashamed of. Her hand strayed to her necklace.

She had come to the art gallery tonight not simply to support Rufus. She had a job to do, she reminded herself.

Crispin had mentioned that a wealthy Arab prince would be attending the exhibition. Apparently Sheikh Mussada enjoyed buying gifts for his new wife, and Tahlia hoped that if she could catch his attention he might be impressed by the sapphire necklace and request to see more Reynolds Gems jewellery. If Reynolds could earn the patronage of an Arab prince they might not need to sell to Vantage Investments after all, she mused, so lost in her thoughts that she did not realise that Crispin had led her into the second gallery until he addressed a man who was studying one of the paintings.

'Thanos—I hope you're enjoying the exhibition. May I introduce you to a fellow art-lover?' Crispin drew Tahlia forward. 'This is Tahlia Reynolds. Her company, Reynolds Gems, have sponsored Rufus throughout his career, and she has an expert knowledge of his work.'

Shock ripped through Thanos as he stared at the woman at Crispin Blythe's side. She had dominated his thoughts for so long that for a few seconds his brain struggled to comprehend that she was standing in front of him, and it took all his formidable will-power to school his expression into one of polite interest rather than murderous rage.

He had arrived in London three days ago, and at a dinner party with friends had been introduced to Crispin, who had invited him to this exhibition at his art gallery. Thanos had no particular interest in art, but these events were always useful for social networking. You never knew who you might meet, he thought derisively, as his eyes raked over Tahlia Reynolds's slender form.

He recognised her instantly. Hardly surprising when her face was plastered over the front of all the red-top tabloids, he thought sardonically. But the photos of her in the newspapers, even the artfully posed pictures in the glossy magazines, showing her in couture gowns and stunning jewellery, did not do justice to her luminescent beauty. His eyes swept over her close-fitting blue silk cocktail dress, which matched the sapphires at her throat and was cut low to reveal a tantalising glimpse of the upper curve of her breasts.

She was exquisite, he acknowledged grimly. He welcomed the wave of black hatred that surged through him, but to his disgust another, unbidden emotion stirred within him. Nothing had prepared him for the impact of seeing Tahlia in the flesh, and to his fury he felt an unmistakable tug of sexual interest.

An awkward silence hovered in the air after Crispin's introduction, and as the gallery-owner cleared his throat Thanos acknowledged that he could not give in to his inclination to fasten his hands around Tahlia's slender neck and squeeze the life from her body.

'Miss Reynolds,' he murmured smoothly, extending his hand to her. He noted that she hesitated before she responded, and her hand shook very slightly when she placed it in his. Her fingers were slim, and as pale as milk. It would take a fraction of his strength to crush them in his grasp. He tightened his grip rather more than was necessary, and when her eyes flew to his face he stared at her impassively.

The brief pressure on her fragile bones could not compare with the pain his sister endured every day, he thought savagely. Melina had been in hospital for six long months, and would have to undergo many more weeks of physiotherapy before she would walk unaided again. Thanos did not blame the driver of the car which had ploughed into Melina. The police had assured him that the man behind the wheel had stood no chance of avoiding the young woman who had run into the road without looking.

No, he held two other people responsible for the accident which had almost ended Melina's life—and those same two people had callously broken her heart. Tahlia Reynolds was a predatory bitch who had been having an affair with Melina's husband, James Hamilton. Melina had been distraught when she had discovered them together in a hotel bedroom, and she had fled outside onto an unlit country road, straight into the path of an oncoming car.

Thanos released Tahlia's hand but continued to scrutinise her intently. According to the recent press reports she had been up to her old tricks with another married actor. Did this woman have *any* scruples? he wondered savagely. How dared she stand there staring at him with her startling bright blue eyes, her mouth curved into a hesitant smile?

Soon she would have little to smile about, he brooded. He had already dealt with his ex-brother-in-law. Immediately after Melina's accident James had fled to L.A., but the actor had quickly discovered that no Hollywood director would work with him after Thanos had threatened to withdraw his financial backing of various film projects if James Hamilton was given so much as a walk-on part. James's acting career was dead and buried, and Thanos was determined that it would never be resurrected. Now he wanted revenge on James's mistress.

Tahlia's hand was still tingling as if she had received an electric shock. Some indescribable force had certainly shot from her fingertips all the way up her arm when she had shaken Thanos Savakis's hand, and now she felt strangely light-headed. The champagne must have gone to her head, she thought ruefully. The peculiar feeling that had swept over her when Thanos's skin had briefly come into contact with hers was *not* an intense reaction to the sexiest man she had ever laid eyes on, she told herself firmly. And yet she could not deny that he unsettled her.

'It's a pleasure to meet you, Mr Savakis,' she said politely. 'Are you here in London on business, or…?' She tailed away uncertainly, entranced by the sudden smile that lifted his features from handsome to breathtakingly gorgeous, and revealed a flash of white teeth which for some inexplicable reason made her think of the story of Red Riding Hood and the cunning wolf.

'Business…and pleasure,' Thanos drawled, relieved that he was once more in control of his hormones. He trailed his eyes over Tahlia. She was exquisitely packaged: designer dress, shoes and handbag, not to mention an eye-watering collection of sapphires and diamonds that sparkled enticingly against her creamy skin. Her outfit must have cost a fortune, he thought cynically. Tahlia was clearly used to the finer things in life, and he was going to take enormous pleasure in putting an end to her pampered, self-indulgent lifestyle.

He had expected her to show some sort of reaction when he introduced himself, but there had been no flicker of response in Tahlia's eyes at the name Savakis. Presumably she had been unaware of James Hamilton's wife's maiden name—no doubt she and James had not spared a thought for Melina during their secret assignations. Molten fury seared his insides. He wanted to vent his anger and denounce her as the heartless whore who had wrecked his sister's life—let the members of London's high society who were gathered in the gallery hear what a cheap little tart she was. But with a huge effort of will he resisted the urge. There would be time enough to tell her what he thought of her after he had brought her to her knees.

'I see that Earl Fullerton has just arrived,' Crispin Blythe murmured. 'I'll leave you two to have fun. I suggest you ask Tahlia to give you a tour of the gallery, Thanos. She has a special relationship with the artist, and is the best person—apart from Rufus himself, of course—to talk about his work.'

'Oh, but…' Tahlia stared after Crispin, unbearably embarrassed by the obvious way he had manoeuvred her and the sexy Greek together. Thanos's mouth was still curved into a smile, but the faintly derisive gleam in his eyes unnerved her, and she could not shake off the idea that for some reason he had taken an instant dislike to her. 'I mustn't monopolise your company, Mr Savakis,' she murmured, glancing rather desperately around the gallery, in the hope that she would spot someone she knew.

'What exactly is the nature of your "special relationship" with Rufus Hartman?' Thanos queried coolly. 'Is he one of your lovers?'

For a moment Tahlia was too taken aback to reply. With a sinking feeling she realised that Thanos had probably seen the newspaper reports of her supposed affair with Damian Casson. Her temper flared. So much for Crispin's assertion that no one believed the rubbish that was written in the downmarket tabloids. 'I really don't see that it's any of your business,' she said coldly, 'but as a matter of fact Rufus isn't attracted to women,' she added. She was not sure why she had lowered her voice, because Rufus was quite open about the fact that he was gay. 'He is a good friend with an incredible talent.'

Thanos's dark eyes roamed lazily over her, as if he were mentally undressing her, and Tahlia felt horribly exposed in her low-cut gown. Her eyes seemed to be drawn to his face of their own volition, and she could not help but focus on the sensual curve of his mouth. His kiss would not be gentle. The thought crashed into her head and her face burned as she imagined him lowering his head and covering her lips with his. Heat coursed through her veins, and when she tore her eyes from him and glanced down she was mortified to see the outline of her nipples clearly visible beneath her dress.

Tahlia had turned her head again, and seemed to be scanning the room for someone. 'Are you searching for anyone in particular?' Thanos queried, his eyes narrowing when she shrugged her slim shoulders. Her skin was so pale it was almost translucent. He noticed a dusting of gold freckles along her collarbone and the slopes of her breasts and felt a tightening sensation in his groin. His fierce awareness of her was both unexpected and infuriating, but it was satisfying to see the evidence that she was equally aware of him.

If she had been any other woman he would have wasted no time in seducing her. With her track record he doubted she would need much persuading into his bed. Disgust swept through him and he ruthlessly banished the image of peeling the straps of her blue silk gown down her shoulders and exposing her slender naked body. She was his brother-in-law's whore, he reminded himself grimly, and it was inconceivable that he could desire her when he had sworn revenge on her for the pain she had caused his sister.

Thanos's accented voice was deep and sensual, and it sent a little shiver of awareness down Tahlia's spine, but she was determined to ignore the effect he had on her. 'I'm looking for an Arab prince—Sheikh Mussada,' she said coolly. 'Do you know him?'

'I know of him—as, I imagine, does everyone else here tonight, seeing that he has recently taken over a major high street bank.'

'Yes, I believe he is the fifth richest man in the world,' Tahlia muttered distractedly, supremely conscious of the exotic scent of Thanos's aftershave. She wondered if it would appear impolite if she walked away from him, and then—recalling his dig about Rufus being 'one of her lovers'—

wondered why she should give a damn what he thought of her. The Prince must have arrived by now, she thought, as she craned her neck to peer into the larger gallery.

Thanos frowned, wondering what had caused the hectic flush on Tahlia's cheeks. 'Didn't Sheikh Mussada marry recently?' he queried tersely, a sudden suspicion forming in his brain.

'Yes, but apparently his wife hates flying, and never travels abroad with him.'

Tahlia thought of the business cards in her purse. As she had driven to the gallery she'd indulged in a daydream in which Sheikh Mussada admired her sapphire necklace and asked her where he could buy something similar. That would be Tahlia's cue to invite him to visit one of the Reynolds Gems shops—she would arrange to open the store out of hours if the Sheikh preferred, and expert assistants would be on hand to help him purchase a gift for his wife. In the daydream, Sheikh Mussada was so impressed by Reynolds' stock of jewellery that he requested their catalogue to take back to Dubai. Soon afterwards they would be flooded with orders from the Prince and his numerous wealthy relatives.

'Oh, that must be him.' Tahlia felt a spurt of excitement as the throng of guests parted and she glimpsed a man wearing traditional Arab robes. This was her chance to save her family's business. The sapphire collection she was wearing tonight was truly spectacular, and Sheikh Mussada was reputed to be an enthusiastic collector of top-quality jewellery. All she had to do was somehow gain his attention.

'Hey, don't run away.'

Warm breath feathered Tahlia's neck, whispering across the stray tendrils of hair at her nape, and she jerked her head around, startled to discover that Thanos had moved and was now standing much too close for comfort.

'Sorry?' For a few seconds she had been so caught up in her daydream about the Sheikh that she had almost forgotten about Thanos. Almost, but not entirely, she conceded ruefully. He was not an easy man to forget, and as she stared at his beautifully sculpted face and glimpsed the flare of sensual heat in his eyes her breath snagged in her throat.

'Our host has assured me you are an expert on Rufus Hartman's work, and I wholeheartedly approve of his suggestion that you should give me a guided tour of the exhibition,' he murmured.

'I assure you I'm no expert,' she replied quickly, feeling as though she were drowning in Thanos's dark eyes. His lashes were ridiculously long for a man, she mused, and his skin gleamed like polished bronze, stretched taut over his magnificent cheekbones. He swamped her senses, and her heart slammed painfully beneath her ribs when he reached out and trailed one finger very lightly down her face.

'Your skin is as soft as satin,' he said, his gravelly accent sending a frisson of awareness down her spine. 'I have to admit that I am captivated by your beauty, Tahlia.'

He had to be kidding, Tahlia decided as she struggled to drag oxygen into her lungs. Surely the sexual hunger blazing in his eyes could not be real, when a few moments ago he had been sending out distinct vibes of barely leashed hostility? She was puzzled by his sudden change of attitude, and even more confused that he was staring at her as if she were his every fantasy rolled into one.

'I…' She seemed to have lost the ability to think. She moistened her parched lips with the tip of her tongue, saw him focus intently on the betraying gesture, and felt liquid heat surge through her veins.

'Why don't we start with the landscape in the corner?' Thanos suggested briskly, and he slid his hand beneath her elbow and steered her firmly across the room—out of Sheikh Mussada's view.

Did she get a kick out of seducing other women's husbands? he wondered furiously. He had noted the determined gleam in her eyes when she'd spotted the Sheikh—the way she had stroked her fingers over the sapphire necklace, drawing attention to her slender throat and the provocative swell of her breasts. Beneath her beautiful shell Tahlia Reynolds possessed a cold and calculating heart. James Hamilton was not blameless, but Thanos was convinced that Tahlia had deliberately seduced his sister's husband—and now she was planning to turn her sorcery on the happily married Sheikh Mussada.

Not if he could help it, he vowed grimly. He was not going to let Tahlia out of his sight for the rest of the evening—even if it meant having to pretend that he had fallen under her spell.

CHAPTER TWO

TAHLIA glanced surreptitiously at the clock on the gallery wall and was shocked to see that almost an hour had passed since Thanos had asked her to act as his guide around the exhibition. She could hardly believe she had spent so long in the exclusive company of the sexiest man in the room, and she could not help but find his attention flattering. His hand was resting lightly in the small of her back, and she was agonisingly aware of his lean, hard body, so close to her that she could feel the warmth that emanated from him and smell the subtle scent of his cologne. He seemed in no hurry for them to part company—but she was supposed to be networking, offering business cards to anyone who admired her necklace. So far she hadn't done a very good job of drumming up new business.

'I'm sure Rufus will be able to discuss his work in far more depth than I can,' she murmured, as Thanos halted in front of a painting that looked as though the artist had flung splodges of vivid colour onto the canvas, and which to Tahlia's eyes did not resemble anything vaguely recognisable.

Thanos followed her gaze across the room to where the long-haired and bearded Rufus Hartman was chatting with a group of guests.

'But he is not nearly such an attractive guide,' he

drawled, a gleam of undisguised sexual interest in his eyes as he turned back to Tahlia, stealing her breath. Thanos Savakis was an outrageous flirt, and her common sense told her she should walk away from him and keep on walking. But her usual caution seemed to have deserted her; she was blown away by his charismatic charm, and when his mouth curved into that devastatingly sexy smile her heart began to race.

Thanos glanced back at the picture. 'Mr Hartman's abstract paintings are the sort of thing I'd like to have in my new hotel. They're contemporary and eye-catching and would suit the modern design of the building.'

'I understand you own a chain of hotels? Crispin mentioned it,' Tahlia admitted, flushing at Thanos's quizzical expression.

What else had Crispin told her? he wondered sardonically. That he was a billionaire with a penchant for blondes? Had Tahlia asked the gallery-owner to introduce them, confident that he would find her red-gold hair and milky-pale skin intriguingly different from the dozens of bleached blonde, sunbed-tanned women who were milling around the gallery, eyeing him rather than the artwork on display?

'I own hotels in many parts of the world, including the Caribbean and the Maldives, and I'm currently in negotiations to buy the Ambassador Hotel, where I am staying on this trip to London.'

Tahlia's eyes widened. The Ambassador was one of the most exclusive hotels in the capital. She had taken little notice when Crispin had said that Thanos was a billionaire, but now it struck her that he could probably buy Reynolds Gems out of his petty cash.

'My latest development is in one of the Greek Islands,' Thanos continued. 'The Artemis is a five-star hotel, offering the ultimate pampering experience—superbly equipped gyms, spas and beauty parlours, together with shops selling designer clothes and jewellery.'

'It sounds wonderful,' Tahlia murmured, her mind focusing on Thanos's mention of jewellery shops within his hotel. Unconsciously her hand strayed to the row of sapphires and diamonds around her neck. The ornate necklace was not the sort of thing she usually wore, but it was undoubtedly impressive, and tonight she needed to impress.

Thanos's gaze followed the movement of her hand. 'Your necklace is almost as exquisite as the woman wearing it,' he remarked.

She blushed. 'It's just one of a wide range of pieces made by the expert goldsmiths and designers at Reynolds Gems. Our gemologists source the finest precious stones and diamonds to ensure that every piece of jewellery is of top quality.' Tahlia hesitated. Was it fair to subject Thanos to the hard sell when they were at a party, not in a boardroom? Their business needed all the help it could get, she reminded herself, and she had to seize every available opportunity to promote the company.

'Perhaps you might like to consider selling a selection of Reynolds Gems jewellery at the Artemis?' she said carefully. She opened her purse and extracted a business card. 'I believe it could be a mutually beneficial arrangement. Reynolds has an excellent reputation for superb craftsmanship, which would be in keeping with the high quality of your hotel. And we are an expanding company,' she added, as Thanos studied the card she had handed him.

'Really…?' He gave her a razor-sharp glance, and Tahlia felt the colour rise in her cheeks.

'Oh, yes. We have a dynamic management team which is always on the look out for exciting new ventures.' That, at least, wasn't a downright lie. She knew her father would jump at the chance to improve Reynolds' profits.

Thanos's slow smile once more sent heat surging through Tahlia's veins, yet at the same time she was again reminded of a wolf stalking its prey.

'That's certainly a very interesting proposition, Tahlia. I'll give your suggestion serious consideration,' he murmured.

'You will?' She forgot that she was supposed to be a hard-headed businesswoman and grinned at him. She felt as though Christmas had come early—and maybe it had, she thought excitedly. Thanos owned up-market hotels around the world, and if he allowed Reynolds Gems to promote their jewellery to his wealthy clientele it could completely turn around the company's fortunes.

Thanos's eyes narrowed on Tahlia's face. Gone was the exquisite and rather haughty-looking socialite. In her place was a young woman with an impish smile and sparkling blue eyes which were more beautiful than the most priceless of sapphires. How could she lie so blatantly and yet look so innocent? And how could he hate her and want her with equal intensity? He despised her, but at this moment he despised himself more—because he could not deny his longing to pull her into his arms and claim her soft, smiling mouth with his lips.

Suddenly he was tired of the game he had been foolish enough to start. He should have revealed from the beginning that he was her lover James Hamilton's ex-brother-in-law. He was tempted to tell Tahlia there was not a chance in hell he would enter into any 'mutually beneficial arrangement' with her or her company, but he swallowed the words. He had laid his plans carefully, and now he was poised to destroy Reynolds Gems. His moment of revenge would be sweet, and he wanted to savour the expression on her beautiful face when she realised that she had lost everything.

There was no reason to remain with her any longer. Sheikh Mussada had left the gallery some fifteen minutes ago, he reminded himself, infuriated by the knowledge that he had prolonged his time with her because he had found her intelligent and witty conversation utterly captivating. He glanced around the gallery and saw that the blonde who had attached herself to him like a limpet when he had first arrived was giving him baleful looks. To his annoyance he could not help but compare Lisette's fluffy platinum blonde curls and her sequined dress with its plunging neckline and thigh high skirt to Tahlia's graceful elegance.

His jaw tightened and he gave Tahlia a cool smile. 'I must ask you to excuse me, Tahlia. I'm expecting a business call and need to return to my hotel.'

'Oh, but…' Tahlia stared at Thanos's retreating form, startled by his abrupt departure. He was striding away across the gallery. She felt embarrassed at the thought of calling him back, but she might never have this opportunity again. 'Can I look forward to hearing from you when you've had time to consider my idea about selling Reynolds Gems jewellery in your new hotel?' she called desperately.

Thanos paused and glanced back at her, his expression unfathomable. 'Oh, you'll certainly be hearing from me, Tahlia,' he promised softly. But for some reason his words sent a frisson of unease down her spine.

Tahlia woke early on Monday morning, with a heavy sense of dread in the pit of her stomach. Today her mother was due to see a specialist, to hear whether a mastectomy followed by a course of chemotherapy had destroyed her breast cancer. In the past few weeks Vivienne had regained some of her strength, and her hair had grown back enough that she no longer needed to wear the brightly coloured silk scarves mother and daughter had chosen together before the start of her treatment.

Her mother had been so brave, Tahlia thought, swallowing the lump in her throat. The past two years since Vivienne had been diagnosed had been a nightmare for both her parents, and she hoped with all her heart that today they would be given the news that she was completely cured.

The future of Reynolds Gems was another worry, she acknowledged grimly as she stepped into the shower. She was not hopeful that Thanos Savakis would agree to promote their jewellery at his new hotel, and if Vantage Investments decided against a buy-out, she did not know what would happen to the company her father had devoted his life to.

She would try and find out more about the situation today, she decided as she applied minimal make-up and swept her hair into a loose knot on top of her head.

The May sunshine streaming through the window was warm enough for her to choose a lightweight outfit. Her pale grey pencil skirt and matching jacket were years old, but the precarious state of her finances meant that new clothes were out of the question. She was grateful that her mother had taught her to choose classics rather than high fashion items, because the suit still looked good, and she teamed it with a lilac blouse, slipped her feet into kitten heels and checked her handbag for lipstick, keys and various other essentials, before hurrying out of her flat, praying that her ancient Mini would start this morning.

Tahlia was puzzled to see her father's car in the car park when she arrived at the Reynolds Gems shop just off Bond Street, and she raced upstairs to the office. 'I wasn't expecting to see you,' she greeted him, her smile fading when she saw the tense expression on Peter Reynolds's face. 'What's wrong?' She paled. 'You can't have heard from the hospital this early?'

'No.' Her father sought to reassure her. 'Your mother's appointment is still scheduled for eleven-thirty. I'm here because I received a call from Vantage Investments at eight o'clock this morning, informing me that they've changed the date of our meeting from Wednesday to midday today.'

'But today is impossible. Ask if we can reschedule for tomorrow.'

'I tried,' her father said wearily. 'But they say we can meet today or not at all.'

'You have to go to the hospital with Mum,' Tahlia said urgently. 'Nothing is more important than her appointment with Mr Rivers. What about asking the hospital if they can rearrange your meeting with him?'

'I've tried that too, but he's flying off to a conference later today.' Peter sighed heavily. 'I hate to put this on you, Tahlia, but I've told Steven Holt from Vantage that we'll go ahead with the meeting, although only one of the directors will be present. This will just be a preliminary meeting, but it sounds as though they are seriously interested in making a deal. Obviously if it all goes to plan I'll be involved in the negotiations, but today it's all down to you. Do you think you can handle it?'

'Of course I can,' Tahlia assured him firmly, her heart contracting when she noted the deep lines furrowing his brow. Her father looked as though he had aged ten years since her mother's illness had been diagnosed, and she was willing to do anything to alleviate his stress. 'Leave the figures for me to read through, and I'll do my best to convince Vantage to buy Reynolds Gems. You need to go home and keep Mum calm before her appointment.' She bit her lip and added huskily, 'Ring me as soon as you have any news, won't you?'

'I will,' her father assured her gravely. 'All the paperwork is on my desk,' he added distractedly, and Tahlia knew that the only thing on his mind right now was her mother.

'Go,' she said gently, giving him a little push towards the door. And with a ghost of a smile he walked out of the office.

Two hours later, Tahlia put down the documents which outlined the company's financial situation and picked up her cup, grimacing when she took a sip of cold coffee. Only a miracle could save them, she acknowledged dully. It was clear that Reynolds Gems' profit margins had been low for the past couple of years, but despite that her father had gone ahead with a costly refit of all three shops, and had had to borrow a huge amount from the bank to do so.

Now, because of the global recession that had affected so many businesses, the bank was demanding that the loan be repaid—and, as was obvious from the figures, Reynolds did not have enough money to clear its debts. Tahlia could see from various letters that her father had pleaded with other banks for help, but in the present financial climate no one was interested in rescuing a failing company.

If she failed to persuade Vantage to buy Reynolds Gems the company would go bankrupt—it was as simple as that, she acknowledged sickly. The responsibility was terrifying, and as she gathered up her briefcase and handbag she felt a churning sensation in her stomach that grew worse as she walked briskly out of the office.

Vantage Investment's offices were in the heart of the city. Tahlia knew that parking would be a nightmare, so instead of driving she took the tube to Cannon Street, arrived much too early for her meeting and had twenty agonising minutes to kill before she finally pushed open the glass doors and walked through the plush reception area, her heels echoing loudly on the marble floor. The receptionist directed her to the lift, and on the journey up to the seventh floor she peered at her reflection in the stainless steel walls. She quickly applied another coat of lipgloss, dismayed to see that her hand was shaking.

'Miss Reynolds? I'm Steven Holt,' a sandy haired man greeted her when she emerged from the lift.

'It's a pleasure to meet you, Mr Holt,' Tahlia returned the greeting with a nervous smile, hiding her surprise that the CEO had met her, rather than his secretary or a junior manager.

He made no further conversation as she followed him along the corridor, and her confusion increased when he ushered her into a room and quietly closed the door after her. She stared blankly at the solid wood. Was she supposed to sit here and wait for him to return? Tension knotted her stomach as she turned into the room, and her heart almost leapt from her chest when she caught sight of the man sitting behind the desk, his broad shoulders and the proud tilt of his head silhouetted against the bright sunshine pouring through the window.

'Mr Savakis?' She halted abruptly and stared at him, her pulse-rate accelerating as her eyes swept over his thick black hair and hard-boned handsome face, then lowered to his impeccably tailored jacket, blinding white shirt and navy silk tie. He was even more gorgeous than the man who had tormented her dreams: a suave, sophisticated billionaire businessman—but what business did he have here at Vantage Investments, with her?

Thanos was watching her impassively, his dark eyes cold and—the word filtered into Tahlia's mind—pitiless. He made no response to her uncertain smile, simply dipped his head to indicate that she should sit down.

His silence unnerved her, and her voice was unnaturally high-pitched when she burst out, 'I don't understand. I'm here for private discussions with Mr Holt.'

'Steven Holt is the chief executive of Vantage Investments, and in ordinary circumstances your discussions would have been with him,' he told her coolly. 'But these are not ordinary circumstances, Tahlia.' For a split second emotion flared in his eyes, and Tahlia caught her breath at the look of simmering fury he directed at her before his lashes fell, masking his expression. 'Vantage is a subsidiary company of Savakis Enterprises.'

'I see,' Tahlia said carefully, shaken by the look he had given her, and utterly bemused by it. 'Then…you must know why I'm here?'

'Oh, yes, Tahlia. I know exactly why you're here,' Thanos leaned back in his seat and brought the tips of his fingers together. He was a remote and forbidding figure, and he made no attempt to disguise the contempt in his eyes as he raked them over Tahlia's designer suit. No wonder Reynolds Gems was in trouble if Tahlia paid herself a salary well above average to finance the luxurious lifestyle she obviously took for granted, he mused cynically.

'You are hoping to persuade me to buy out your company and save it from bankruptcy. The same company that you assured me is an expanding operation with a dynamic management team,' he said mockingly.

Tahlia felt her cheeks burn as she recalled her suggestion that he might consider allowing Reynolds Gems to sell their jewellery at his new hotel. Clearly he had never had any intention of taking the idea seriously. For some reason he had just been playing her along, and the knowledge sparked her temper.

'Why didn't you tell me of your connection with Vantage Investments, instead of letting me believe there might be a way to save Reynolds?' she demanded angrily. 'Did you enjoy making a fool of me?'

'I admit I found the situation mildly amusing.'

The expression in his eyes chilled her to the bone. 'But why?' she choked. 'What have I ever done to—?' She broke off and stared at the photograph of a young woman that he had pushed across the desk—for a second her heart stopped beating.

'I believe you have met my sister?' Thanos asked, in a dangerously soft tone.

'I…' Tahlia groped for words, her brain in freefall.

'I imagine it was not a long meeting. And there would have been a certain awkwardness to the situation, seeing that you were in bed with Melina's husband at the time. Of course my sister no longer looks as she does in that photo,' Thanos went on, in the same chilling tone of barely suppressed aggression. 'And it is unlikely she will ever dance again—which is a pity because, as you can see from the picture, she loved to dance.'

Tahlia could not formulate a reply as she stared at the photograph of the beautiful young woman whose face was so shockingly familiar. In the picture her dark hair was swept up into a chignon, rather than falling in a mass of curls around her shoulders as it had been on the night Tahlia had seen her, but there was no mistaking that this was James's wife.

'Melina was distraught after she caught you and Hamilton together. She fled from the hotel, and as she dashed across the road she was hit by a car,' Thanos said harshly. 'Eyewitnesses said she was thrown at least twenty feet into the air before she hit the ground. She was in a coma for three weeks, both her legs were broken, and she suffered spinal damage.' He ignored Tahlia's horrified gasp and went on remorselessly, 'For a while the doctors believed she would be in a wheelchair for the rest of her life. Thankfully her last round of surgery was successful, and she is having intensive physiotherapy to help her to walk, but she will never dance again,' he finished grimly, a nerve flickering in his cheek as he picked up the photo of his sister and stared at it.

The silence in the room screamed with tension, until at last Tahlia forced herself to speak. 'I…I didn't know,' she whispered.

Thanos gave a savage laugh. 'You mean you didn't hear the ambulance sirens? Or you did hear them but you were not sufficiently interested to go and find out who had been injured? Presumably you and Hamilton continued with your sexual gymnastics after Melina left?' he snarled contemptuously. 'Neither of you had the decency to follow her, even though it must have been obvious—even to a heartless bitch like you—that she was devastated at finding the man she loved in bed with his whore.'

Tahlia bowed her head while Thanos's savage fury crashed over her. His anger was no less than she deserved, she acknowledged sickly, and her mind relived that terrible night six months ago, which had started off so wonderfully.

She had felt excited and a little nervous when James had checked them in to the hotel he had booked for a romantic weekend.

'Just one key?' she'd queried tremulously, her heart thumping.

'One key, one room—one bed,' he'd replied, with that disarming grin that melted her heart. 'You know I love you, Tahlia,' he had murmured when they'd reached their suite, and he had pulled her into his arms and kissed her. 'And you love me—don't you, baby? Making love is the next step in showing our love for each other.'

She had been unable to resist him: good-looking, easygoing James, who had swept her off her feet. She had been ready for them to become lovers, and when James had started to undress her she had not hidden her eagerness. But as they had tumbled onto the bed the door had burst open, and a woman had stumbled into the room.

She would never forget the look of shock on the woman's face, the tears streaming down her cheeks and her voice crying brokenly, 'How could you, James? How could you? I am your *wife*…'

'I didn't know about your sister's accident,' she insisted shakily, dragging her mind back to the present. 'I left James almost immediately.' After his sulky confirmation that, yes, he *was* married—'but that's no reason to get hysterical, Tahlia.' 'I ran down to my car, parked at the rear of the hotel. Melina must have run out of the front of the hotel, and I drove home along a different road. I don't remember hearing sirens or anything—but I was in shock,' Tahlia said falteringly, remembering how she had driven away, desperately trying to hold back her tears until she reached her parents' home. 'I had no idea that James was married.'

'*Liar.*'

The solitary word cracked through the air like a whip, and Tahlia jumped. 'I swear I didn't know—' she began, but Thanos silenced her with a savage glare.

'Of course you knew. Just as you knew that the actor you've been having an affair with recently was married. Far from attempting to hide your relationship with him, you brazenly flaunted it, allowing yourself to be snapped by the press leaving a hotel with him.' Thanos's lip curled. 'Tell me, do you enjoy a feeling of power when you have sex with other women's husbands? Women like you disgust me.'

Women like his father's mistress, Thanos brooded grimly. Wendy Jones had known that his father had a wife and children, but that had not stopped her flirting with Kosta Savakis and pursuing him with single-minded determination, uncaring of the pain and destruction their affair caused. Wendy and Tahlia were two of a kind—predatory, heartless bitches who lacked any moral decency. His hatred of the woman who had become his stepmother had burned inside him for years, and as he stared across his desk at Tahlia's pale face his fury threatened to choke him.

The icy anger in Thanos's eyes sent a shiver down Tahlia's

spine, and she said frantically, 'I promise you I did *not* know James was married. If I had I would never have dated him, let alone agreed to spend a weekend with him.' She jumped to her feet and gripped the edge of the desk, breathing hard so that her breasts rose and fell jerkily. 'When your sister burst into the hotel room and announced that she was James's wife I felt *terrible*. I felt as though I were the lowest life form on the planet.'

'An apt description,' Thanos snapped, his jaw hardening. 'And I have no doubt that you felt terrible—you'd just been caught out, and you knew James was likely to end his affair with you so that he could try and persuade his wealthy wife to forgive him. I don't understand what you saw in my brother-in-law,' he added scathingly. 'James Hamilton is a penniless, talentless waste of space. But, according to the press reports, you seem to get a kick out of sleeping with other women's husbands.'

The colour leached from Tahlia's face, and for a second she was tempted to flee from the room, but she forced herself to meet Thanos's cold stare. 'The reports in the tabloids about my supposed affair with Damian Casson are a complete fabrication,' she said stiltedly. 'And I have instructed my solicitor to proceed with legal action against the papers involved.' Her eyes dropped to the photograph of Thanos's sister and she swallowed. 'I am so sorry,' she whispered. 'I wish I could apologise to Melina, and explain to her that James deceived both of us.'

'Do you think I would allow you anywhere near my sister?' Thanos demanded harshly. 'Melina has suffered enough, without having to hear your lies.'

He had also risen to his feet, and was surveying her with visible contempt. She could understand why he was angry, Tahlia conceded, but his refusal to listen to her and his determination to believe the worst of her sparked her temper.

'I am not lying,' she told him with quiet dignity. 'And I am not the woman portrayed by the tabloids. I had no idea that James had a wife.' Tears stung her eyes, and she lowered her head so that Thanos would not see them. She had felt a fool that night in the hotel, when James's treachery had been revealed, but her emotions were of little significance compared to the pain—both mental and physical—that Thanos's sister must be suffering.

'I'm so sorry,' she repeated shakily. She had been an innocent pawn in James's game, but she still felt responsible for his wife's terrible accident.

'It's too damned late to be sorry,' Thanos grated. 'It's a pity you did not feel this touching remorse *before* you slept with my sister's husband.'

'I never slept with him,' Tahlia said quickly. 'Although I realise that will be small comfort to Melina. I admit that I had intended to become James's lover. The night that Melina found us at the hotel would have been our first night together.' She swallowed, but forced herself to go on, aware that Thanos and his sister deserved her honesty. 'I had fallen in love with James—although I realise now that I never really knew him at all,' she added bitterly.

She was good, Thanos conceded grimly. She almost had him convinced that she was as innocent as she protested—and the shimmer of tears in those beautiful blue eyes was a nice touch. If it wasn't for the story in the tabloids about her affair with another married actor he might have been tempted to believe her.

But perhaps he *wanted* to believe that Tahlia had been hoodwinked by James Hamilton because of his own inconvenient physical attraction to her? he brooded irritably. Today she was the epitome of understated elegance: her slim-fitting skirt skimmed the gentle flare of her hips, and the cut of her jacket emphasised her tiny waist, while her soft lilac-coloured blouse complemented her creamy complexion. The scattering of freckles across her nose and cheeks matched her red-gold hair, while the long lashes fringing those startlingly blue eyes were a slightly darker shade of gold.

She might be lovely on the outside, but inside she was rotten to the core, and all the evidence proved that she had known just what she was doing when she began her affair with James, Thanos reminded himself. He was not going to be duped by her lies simply because his hormones were raging out of control. His mouth tightened and he forced himself to move away from her, strolling across the room to stare out of the window at the view of the city.

Tahlia watched him, her eyes roaming over his broad shoulders and the arrogant tilt of his head. Despair settled like a lead weight in her stomach.

'You never had any intention of buying out Reynolds Gems, did you?' she said dully.

'None whatsoever,' he replied coolly. 'It seemed entirely fair that you should suffer a fraction of the misery my sister has suffered, and so I decided to destroy your company. But, to be honest, bringing about Reynolds Gems' downfall has not been difficult. Some of the decisions taken by the company during the last two years have been downright reckless, and they are directly responsible for Reynolds' current financial situation. I simply tricked you into thinking that Vantage Investments would offer a rescue package, and you were gullible enough— or more likely greedy enough—to be fooled into believing you could hang on to your self-indulgent lifestyle.'

It was no coincidence that Reynolds Gems' problems had begun at the same time as her mother's illness had been diagnosed, Tahlia acknowledged. During that terrible time business had come a long way down her father's list of priorities, and she felt guilty that she had not become more involved with running the company.

'Reynolds Gems is my father's company, not mine,' she said quietly. 'If you destroy it you will be hurting him.'

'You became a partner three years ago. My investigations were very thorough,' Thanos said coldly, turning away from the window to give her a sardonic look. 'It's too bad your father will lose the company he built from scratch, but he shouldn't have brought his daughter up to be an immoral slut.'

Anger, swift and white-hot, churned inside Tahlia. Her eyes flew to the clock above the desk and she felt a pang of dread. Had her mother been told that her battle with breast cancer had been successful? Or, as the specialist had warned might happen, had the cancer spread? Even if the news was bad, her father would hide his fears and support Vivienne, just as he had done every day for the past two years. Only Tahlia knew that sometimes he sat alone in his study and wept. Peter Reynolds, of all people, did not deserve Thanos's disdain.

Shaking with fury, she marched across the office and stood directly in front of Thanos. 'Think what you like about me, but don't you *dare* say a word against my father. He is a better man than you will ever be.'

'Not in business,' Thanos drawled sarcastically.

Tahlia flushed. 'I accept he had made some unwise decisions, but there were reasons…' She glanced at Thanos's mocking expression and halted abruptly. She refused to discuss her mother's health problems with him when she was sure he would accuse her of lying to gain his sympathy. Her anger dissipated as quickly as it had arrived, leaving her feeling drained and despairing as the realisation hit her that there was no hope of saving Reynolds Gems from the administrators.

'I wish more than anything that I'd never met James

Hamilton,' she said huskily. 'And I hope with all my heart that your sister makes a full recovery.'

She swung away from him, choking back the tears she was determined would not fall until she was outside his office. Her knee collided painfully with the coffee table.

'Damn it!' She stumbled, dropped her briefcase, and bit back an oath as it burst open and spilled its contents over the floor.

No doubt Thanos was enjoying seeing her on her knees, she thought furiously, as she knelt and began to scoop up the pages of figures that spelled the demise of Reynolds Gems. She dashed her hand over her eyes and froze when she realised that he had crouched beside her and was helping to gather up her paperwork.

'Thank you.' She took the papers he handed her and slowly lifted her head, startled to find him so close. The tang of his cologne drifted around her, teasing her senses, and she could feel the dry heat emanating from his body. How could she be so agonisingly aware of him when he had made it clear that he despised her? she wondered despairingly.

It was suddenly imperative that she stood up and moved away from him, before he realised the effect he had on her, but her muscles had seized up. Her eyes were drawn to his—and shock ricocheted through her when she glimpsed the un-mistakable feral desire blazing in their depths.

CHAPTER THREE

How could he feel this overwhelming sexual attraction to Tahlia when he loathed her? Thanos wondered furiously. His brain acknowledged that she was an immoral slut, but his body was responding with humiliating eagerness to the delicate fragrance of her perfume. He could not tear his eyes from the soft curve of her mouth, and the tantalising fullness of her lips was proving an irresistible temptation. His desire for her was an unexpected complication that filled him with self-disgust, but no amount of reminding himself of Melina's injuries could banish the fierce urge to crush Tahlia's lips beneath his.

Thanos was going to kiss her. Tahlia saw the smouldering intent in his eyes seconds before he lowered his head, and she was stunned by the realisation that she wanted him to. He believed she had slept with his sister's husband, and he had made his opinion of her quite clear, but for reasons she could not understand she made no attempt to deny him and simply waited, heart thumping, for his mouth to claim hers.

The first brush of his mouth sent a quiver of reaction through her. His lips were firm, sliding demandingly over hers, but Tahlia's pride belatedly came to her aid and she clamped her mouth shut, fighting the overwhelming temptation to respond to him. He hated her, she reminded herself. And he thought he had good reason to destroy Reynolds Gems in a bid to hurt her. He adamantly refused to believe that she had not set out to deliberately steal his sister's husband, and if she gave in to the urgent clamouring of her body and kissed him back it would surely confirm his belief that she was the immoral slut he had accused her of being.

But she had recognised the sizzling sexual chemistry between them at the art gallery, and now it was raging out of control, consuming them both. When he caught hold of her hand and drew her to her feet she went unresistingly—now they were standing so close, yet not quite touching, and her senses were inflamed by the subtle scent of male pheromones, the intoxicating heat emanating from his hard body that made her long to close the gap between them and have him crush her against his muscular chest.

His lips hardened, became more urgent, and her will-power crumbled beneath the onslaught. With a little gasp she opened her mouth, and he immediately thrust his tongue deep into its moist warmth, exploring her with shocking eroticism as he snaked his arm around her waist and jerked her close, hip to hip, her soft breasts pressed against his rock-solid body.

His hungry passion was like nothing she had ever experienced before, and it drove every thought from her head other than her frantic need for him to continue kissing her. She forgot that they were standing in his office, forgot that he owned Vantage Investments and had refused to save Reynolds Gems from collapse. She was only aware of him, of the demanding pressure of his lips and the faint abrasion of his jaw against the softer skin of her cheek as he angled her head and deepened the kiss to another level that was flagrantly erotic.

She was aware of the melting warmth between her thighs, and the rigid proof of his arousal pressing into her belly. With a low moan of capitulation she moved her hands to his shoulders. She would have wound her arms around his neck, but he abruptly snatched his mouth from hers and jerked his head back, his eyes glittering with contempt as he stared down at her.

'What's the matter Tahlia—has Damian Casson come to his senses and dumped you in favour of his wife? Surely you won't find *me* a good substitute to relieve your sexual frustrations when you're only attracted to married men?' he taunted, his voice dripping with sarcasm that made her skin crawl.

Tahlia gasped, and acting purely on impulse she raised her arm and cracked her hand across his cheek. 'You arrogant bastard,' she choked, shaking with anger and humiliation. '*You* kissed *me*. What were you trying to do—prove how irresistible you are?'

'I certainly proved something,' Thanos drawled as he strolled back across the room and leaned his hip against his desk, folding his arms across his chest in an indolent stance that disguised the fact that his heart was slamming beneath his ribs. 'The sexual alchemy between us is as potent as it is inexplicable, and I admit I kissed you because I was curious to see how you would react.' His eyes narrowed on her white face. 'Hit me again and I promise you will regret it.'

Tahlia stared at the livid red mark on his cheek and felt sick. She had never struck another human being in her life, and she was shocked and ashamed by her violent display of temper. It was no good reminding herself that Thanos had deserved it. He had kissed her, but she had wanted him to, she owned miserably. Despite knowing his low opinion of her, she had been unable to resist him. What did that say about her morals? she wondered despairingly.

Thanos kept his expression deliberately blank, giving no clue to the internal battle raging inside him as he sought to bring his hormones back under control. Kissing her had been a mistake, he acknowledged grimly. He was furious with himself for succumbing to the temptation of her lush mouth, and his temper was not improved by the knowledge that he wanted to kiss her again, to slide his lips down her throat to the pulse beating frenetically at its base, then tug the pins from her hair and run his fingers through the pale red silk.

He studied her dispassionately, wondering if the tears clinging like tiny sparkling diamonds to her lashes were meant to make him feel remorse or pity. He felt neither. She deserved to lose her company, and she would still not suffer a fraction of the trauma his sister had suffered.

He had planned Tahlia's downfall during the endless days and nights he had sat at Melina's bedside, waiting for her to regain consciousness. He had felt so helpless and so afraid, he remembered grimly. He who had never feared anything, who had fought his way out of poverty to the pinnacle of success, had been scared that he was going to lose the one person in the world he truly loved. Now Melina was out of danger, and slowly recovering from her injuries, but he would never forget the accident that had so nearly claimed her life— and he would never forgive the two people he deemed responsible for it.

In the current financial climate Tahlia would never find another buyer for Reynolds Gems. Everything was going just as he had planned. But that was not entirely true, he acknowledged irritably. He could not remember the last time he had wanted a woman as badly as he wanted Tahlia and his hunger for her angered him. He had first-hand proof that she was a woman like his father's mistress, yet still he was consumed with this damnable longing to possess her.

Maybe he should seize what he wanted and be damned, he mused grimly. He had planned to take revenge for his sister by fooling Tahlia into believing that his company would buy

Reynolds Gems and then withdrawing his offer of financial support at the last minute. He had no interest in saving Reynolds' three failing jewellery shops, but those shops *were* in prime London locations. The current recession meant that the property market had all but collapsed; he knew Peter Reynolds had tried and failed to sell the shops, and that now his creditors had run out of patience, but eventually the financial climate would improve and the shops would be lucrative investments.

Thanos's business brain told him he would be a fool to turn down the opportunity to increase his property portfolio—and wouldn't his revenge be all the sweeter if he made it personal? Buying out Reynolds Gems would save Tahlia from financial ruin, but he would demand repayment in full—in his bed!

The tense silence stretched Tahlia's nerves, and her skin prickled beneath Thanos's intent gaze. He appeared relaxed, but he reminded her of a panther: sleek, dark and dangerous as it eyed its prey. She had to get out of his office, she thought wildly. Gather what little dignity she had left and leave.

She retrieved her briefcase from the floor, where she had dropped it, and turned towards the door.

'There might be a way I could be persuaded to buy Reynolds Gems…'

His soft drawl stopped her in her tracks, and she swung back to face him, her heart thumping. It was probably a trick, she told herself, or a joke at her expense, but she was desperate for a lifeline—however tenuous.

'How?' she demanded baldly.

'The time-honoured tradition of bartering—each of us has something the other wants,' he elucidated, when she stared at him blankly. 'It's possible we could negotiate a deal.'

Tahlia frowned. 'What do I have that you want? I have nothing.'

Dark eyes burned into her, and she felt a fierce tugging sensation deep in her pelvis. 'Don't be naïve, Tahlia,' he said, in a faintly bored tone. 'You know perfectly well what I want.' He crossed the room in two strides and slid his hand beneath her chin, holding her prisoner and forcing her to meet his gaze. *'You,'* he said bluntly. 'I want to take you to bed and enjoy the delectable body that you share so willingly with your numerous lovers.' He ignored her gasp of outrage and continued coolly. 'In return for your sexual favours I am prepared to buy Reynolds Gems for the full asking price.'

A bubble of hysteria rose in Tahlia's throat. She had been right; it *was* a cruel joke. But there had been no hint of amusement in Thanos's voice, and the feral heat in his eyes scorched her skin. 'But…you don't like me,' she faltered, picking from the random threads of thought that whirled in her head.

That did seem to amuse him, and he laughed derisively. 'It is not necessary for me to *like* you. I want to have sex with you; I'm not suggesting that we become best friends.'

Tahlia flushed at his mockery. 'I have always thought that lovers should also be friends.' Thanos could not have made it clearer that he was only interested in using her body for his sexual satisfaction. 'I am not a piece of meat,' she told him scathingly, 'and I am not for sale.'

Thanos's eyes narrowed. How dared Tahlia speak to him in that contemptuous tone when, according to the press reports, she dropped her knickers for any Z-list celebrity who gave her the time of day?

'Everything and everyone is for sale for the right price,' he told her mockingly. 'You should be grateful of my offer. Who else do you think will be prepared to shell out a six-figure sum for a failing company? That's a damn good rate for even the most inventive hooker. And besides,' he drawled, tightening his grip on her chin when she tried to jerk out of his grasp, 'we both know you would not find it such an ordeal to share my bed. You might want to deny the sexual chemistry that burns between us, but your body is more honest.'

At that moment Tahlia would have given her life to deny his sardonic taunt, but from the moment he had moved close to her the exotic tang of his aftershave, mixed with another subtle masculine scent, had pervaded her senses and lit a flame inside her. Her breasts felt heavy, and she caught her breath when he trailed his free hand down her front and discovered the hard peaks of her nipples jutting beneath her silk blouse.

Anger was her only weapon against the insidious warmth that licked through her veins. He thought she was no better than a prostitute. She would not, *could* not give in to the voice in her head which urged her to agree to his outrageous proposal. It would be devastating to lose Reynolds Gems, but far worse to sacrifice her pride and her self-respect.

'Hell will freeze over before I agree to your disgusting suggestion,' she snapped.

He shrugged. 'Are you prepared to stand by and allow your father to lose the company he has devoted his life to for the past thirty years?'

Tahlia swallowed the lump that had formed in her throat. 'Emotional blackmail is despicable. My father would never expect me to sell my body, even if it means losing everything he owns. You seem to think that your wealth gives you special privileges. Obviously you were born with a silver spoon in your mouth,' she flung at him, remembering that Crispin Blythe had said that Thanos was a billionaire. 'You believe your money can buy you anything. But it can't buy me.'

'In that case I may as well take what you give away freely to so many other men,' he bit out savagely, seizing her shoulders and slamming her against his chest. He lowered his head and captured her mouth with bruising force. Tahlia gave a shocked cry, and he took advantage of her parted lips to thrust his tongue between them, exploring her with a bold eroticism that made her tremble. Anger came to her rescue and she pushed against his chest, but he merely tightened his arms around her until she felt as though she were trapped in a vice. She was determined not to respond to him, but he seemed to sense her resolve and eased the pressure of his mouth a fraction, changing the kiss from one of domination to a sensual tasting that she found utterly irresistible.

She felt as though her bones were dissolving. Her legs no longer seemed capable of bearing her weight, and she sagged against him, relaxing her balled fists and splaying her hands over his chest, feeling the heat of his body through his shirt. She felt his fingers slide up her nape and with a deft movement he released the pins from her chignon so that her hair uncoiled and fell in a scented silky curtain around her shoulders. He made a muffled noise in his throat and buried his hands in her hair, angling her head while he deepened the kiss. She responded helplessly, closing her eyes as she sank deeper into the velvet softness of his caress.

Lost in a world of sensory pleasure, she was unprepared when he suddenly lifted his head and stared down at her. The cold contempt in his dark eyes doused her in a wave of humiliation as she realised that she was clinging to him.

'My offer still stands,' he said coolly.

She jerked away from him, tears of shame burning her eyes. There was no evidence in his mocking expression that he had been stirred by the kiss, while *she* was a seething mass of emotions and could not disguise the effect he had on her.

'My answer is still the same,' she said curtly. 'I am not for sale.'

She was sure he would taunt her with the fact that she had offered no resistance when he had kissed her again, but he shrugged uninterestedly and flicked back his cuff to glance at his watch.

'In that case I believe we have covered everything,' he said coolly. 'Perhaps you'll have better luck securing a rescue plan for Reynolds Gems elsewhere?'

He must know that her father had approached a number of banks for help and had been refused. But pleading with him would be utterly pointless, and would decimate what little dignity she had left. Somehow she forced her limbs to move, snatched up her briefcase, and even managed to bid him a cool goodbye before she swept out of his office with her head held high, determined to deny him the pleasure of witnessing her utter devastation.

Tahlia caught the tube back to Bond Street on auto-pilot, stunned by the events that had taken place in Thanos's office. She could not believe he had made the foul suggestion that she should sleep with him in return for him buying Reynolds Gems. When she had first met him at the art gallery her instincts had warned her that he was ruthless, but now she knew just what kind of a man he was: a man who would pay for sex with a woman who he had admitted he despised. Unquestionably she had made the right decision when she had turned him down. There was no way on earth she would ever agree to be Thanos Savakis's whore. She was furious with herself for allowing him to kiss her—and worse by far was the fact that while she had been in his arms she had forgotten everything—even her mother.

Her phone rang as she walked into her office, and her heart lurched when she saw that the caller was her father. 'Is it good news?' she asked him tensely, hardly daring to breathe as she waited for his reply.

'The best,' he assured her gently. 'The consultant gave your mother the all-clear.'

Tahlia could hear the relief in Peter Reynolds's voice, and tears stung her eyes. 'Thank God,' she whispered shakily. 'Mum must be overjoyed.'

'We both are,' Peter said in a choked voice. 'We're going out to dinner tonight to celebrate—my credit card can just about take it. Will you come?' He hesitated, and then added, 'There's something I need to discuss with you.'

'Of course I'll come,' Tahlia agreed, puzzled by her father's tone. Her mother had beaten cancer and the world was suddenly a wonderful place, so why did he sound so tense? 'Dad, what's the matter?'

There was another long pause before Peter spoke. 'I've had a letter from the bank, threatening to repossess Carlton House.'

'What?' Tahlia's legs gave way and she dropped onto a chair. 'What do you mean? I don't understand. How can the bank repossess Carlton when you and Mum jointly own it?'

'I had to remortgage the house as well as take the loan when we refurbished the shops,' Peter explained flatly. 'Your mother agreed to it because I assured her it was just a temporary solution to a cashflow problem with the company, and she thinks I've already repaid it. I was hoping the bank would give me some leeway, but I'm behind with the repayments and they are demanding I pay the arrears immediately. 'There's no money left, Tahlia. I've used every penny of my personal savings trying to keep Reynolds afloat. I hope to God Vantage Investments are serious about buying Reynolds Gems,' he said thickly, 'because if not I will be solely responsible for losing Carlton and breaking your mother's heart. How did the meeting go?' he asked; a note of desperation audible in his voice. 'Steven Holt sounded pretty keen when I spoke to him a few days ago.'

Tahlia's brain seemed to have stopped functioning. Her parents could not lose Carlton House. It was inconceivable.

In her mind she pictured the graceful old manor house that had been built during the reign of Elizabeth I and which had been passed down through her mother's family for generations. The house was a listed building and had been a serious drain on her parents' finances for years, but they had swiftly dismissed any idea that they might be better to sell Carlton and move to a smaller house which required less upkeep.

Her mother would be utterly heartbroken if she was forced to move from the home she loved now, and after the past two gruelling years of fear and chemotherapy she did not deserve to suffer further misery.

'Yes.' She uttered the word instinctively, because she could not bring herself to say no—to reveal that the meeting had not gone as she or her father had expected, and that the CEO of Vantage Investments had been instructed to sound enthusiastic about buying out Reynolds by Thanos Savakis, head of Vantage's parent company Savakis Enterprises, a man whose only agenda was revenge.

'As you said, it was only a preliminary meeting. There are still a few points to discuss before a buy-out is absolutely certain. Leave things with me while you concentrate on Mum,' she added hurriedly. 'Why don't you take her to Cornwall and stay with Aunt Jess for a few days? You could both do with a break, and Jess would love to see you both.'

She gripped the phone, willing herself to remain calm. 'Dad…you're not serious about the possibility of losing Carlton, are you? I mean, there has to be a way…'

'The only way I can settle the debt on the house is by selling the company,' Peter said flatly. 'A while back there were a couple of other firms who were interested in buying Reynolds, but I turned them down because Vantage Investments offered the best deal. If Vantage should change their mind I'm sunk. The bank is putting pressure on me, and there's no time to find a new buyer. You say that a few things need to be ironed out? I think I should call Steven Holt.'

'*No.*' Tahlia fought to keep the panic from her voice. If her father phoned Vantage he would learn from Thanos that there was no deal and never had been, that the offer to buy Reynolds had just been part of a cruel trick designed to punish *her*. This was her fault, she thought despairingly. If Vantage had not approached her father he would have sold Reynolds to one of the other firms who had been interested, and Carlton House would be safe.

'*Are you prepared to stand by and allow your father to lose the company…?*' Thanos's voice mocked her. The thought had torn her apart, but she had rejected his solution, vowing to find another way to save Reynolds. The defeated note in her father's voice now made it clear there was no other way. It was not simply the company that was in danger but Carlton House, and her parents' happiness and peace of mind.

'*Each of us has something the other wants.*' Thanos was a billionaire who had the means to buy Reynolds, and in return he wanted…

A tremor ran through her. He wanted to have sex with her. She couldn't do it, she thought wildly. But hard on the heels of that thought came the acknowledgement that she had no choice. Her father had admitted he was at rock bottom, and she was at the limit on her own overdraft and credit cards. She could not raise enough money to cover one mortgage repayment on Carlton, let alone clear the arrears.

'There are just a couple of minor points that need clarification before Vantage agrees to the deal,' she told her father, forcing herself to sound calm. 'I'll get back to them and sort it out. Can I speak to Mum?' she asked quickly, before her father could argue.

'Oh, yes—of course…' There was a moment's silence, and then Vivienne's voice sounded down the line.

'Tahlia! Isn't it wonderful?' she said tremulously. 'I feel as though I've been given a second chance at life.'

The raw emotion in her mother's voice tore at Tahlia's heart, and she swallowed the tears that clogged her throat. 'I hope you enjoy every minute of it, Mum,' she whispered. 'You and Dad deserve to be happy.'

And she would do everything in her power to help them, she vowed fiercely as she put down the phone. Even the unthinkable.

Thanos emerged from the *en suite* bathroom and padded across the bedroom to answer the phone, his brows lowering in a frown as he listened to the message relayed by the receptionist. He hesitated for a few moments, wondering why Tahlia Reynolds was standing in the lobby of his hotel at eleven o'clock at night, and silently acknowledged that he was intrigued.

'Inform Miss Reynolds that I will see her in my suite in fifteen minutes,' he murmured, before he replaced the receiver. It wouldn't hurt Tahlia to cool her heels, and if the reason for her unexpected visit was sufficiently important she would wait until he was ready to see her. He also needed to get dressed—unless he intended to greet her wearing nothing but a towel around his hips. When he recalled his body's involuntary reaction to her at their last meeting it was clear that clothes were a necessity, he conceded, his mouth curving into a self-derisive grimace.

To his annoyance his curiosity grew over the following quarter of an hour, and after pouring himself a liberal malt Scotch he paced restlessly around his suite. What did Tahlia want? Had she, after all, decided to offer her body in return for him saving her father from financial ruin? His mouth twisted as he recalled her scathing refusal to sell herself to him earlier in the day. Her reaction had surprised him, he acknowledged. He had first-hand evidence that she had the morals of an alley cat, and the recent story of her affair with another married actor was not the first time her love-life had been reported in the press.

He had been certain that she would agree to sleep with him in return for his agreement to buy Reynolds Gems, but instead she had looked as scandalised as if she were a vestal virgin—which was a laughable notion, he thought sardonically.

'Hell will freeze over before I agree to your disgusting suggestion,' she'd flung at him with icy scorn. So why was she here now? Undoubtedly she wanted something. In his experience women always did, he thought cynically. He stared out of the window at the night-time view of London: the myriad lights of buildings and cars glowing like bright jewels against the black velvet sky, the illuminated London Eye sparkling like an enormous static Catherine wheel. His mind flew back six months to another hotel—this time in Athens—and another woman whose visit had been unexpected.

He had been shocked when Yalena had phoned him out of the blue and suggested they meet up. Fifteen years had passed since the woman he had loved had broken off their engagement and married his best friend, and he admitted he had been curious to gauge his reaction when he met Yalena and Takis again. But Yalena had come to his hotel alone, dressed like a tart and clearly confident that Thanos would not turn down her offer to leave her husband for him. She had made a mistake all those years ago, she had told him tearfully. She realised now that she loved him, not Takis—although Thanos noted that she had only arrived at that conclusion since his name had been included on the list of the world's top one hundred richest men.

Yalena had been dismissive of the fact that her husband

adored her, and worked hard to give her a good lifestyle, and Thanos had felt a mixture of disgust and disappointment that he had been so wrong about her. For years he had put her on a pedestal—the discovery that she was an avaricious gold-digger, just like every other woman he had ever met, had filled him with contempt and the bitter realisation that he had been a fool to waste his emotions on her.

The knock on the door dragged him from his memories. Tahlia was here. He finished the whisky, savouring its warmth as it slid down his throat. What would he do if she *had* come to offer herself to him? He felt a tightening sensation in his groin, and his nostrils flared as sexual heat flooded through him. He wanted her badly, and he could afford her. Why not indulge himself? he brooded. He hadn't had sex for months. Combining visiting Melina in hospital with running a billion-pound company had meant that he'd had neither the time nor the inclination for his usual meaningless sexual liaisons with lovers who knew better than to expect commitment from him. Celibacy did not suit him, he owned as he strode across the suite. His body felt taut, hungry for satisfaction, and antici-pation licked in his veins.

The door of Thanos's suite swung open and Tahlia wondered if he could hear her heart beating frantically against her ribs.

'Tahlia,' he greeted her coolly.

His heavily accented voice caused a delicious little shiver to run down her spine, and at the same time exacerbated the tension that had shredded her nerves during the fifteen minutes she had been forced to wait downstairs in the bar. He stood back for her to enter, and for a few seconds her resolve wobbled, and she was tempted to turn tail and flee. But somehow her legs continued to propel her forward—like a lamb into the wolf's lair, the voice in her head whispered as she moved into the centre of the room. Another tremor ran through her when she heard the click of the door closing behind her.

'You are the mistress of surprise,' Thanos drawled as he strolled towards her.

'What do you mean?' she queried sharply, colour storming into her cheeks. The word *mistress* touched a raw nerve. Thanos believed she had been James Hamilton's mistress. He assumed that she was sexually experienced. The fact that she was not made what she was about to do even harder.

'I did not expect to see you at the art gallery, and I did not anticipate you turning up here tonight.' Nor had he anticipated his reaction to her when he had opened the door—the way his heart had slammed in his chest at the sight of her, looking utterly exquisite in the same blue silk gown she had been wearing the other evening. His desire for her weakened him, and he resented the effect she had on him. 'What do you want, Tahlia?' he demanded tersely, moving away from her to avoid the subtle drift of her perfume that teased his senses.

Tahlia shot him a quick glance that encompassed his black silk shirt, open at the throat to reveal a few inches of bronzed skin covered with crisp, dark hairs, and his superbly tailored black trousers which drew her attention to his lean hips and muscular thighs. The table lamps placed strategically around the room emitted a soft apricot glow that threw his sculpted cheekbones into sharp relief and danced across his gleaming jet-black hair.

He was unfairly gorgeous, and her stomach muscles clenched as she relived those moments in his office when he had crushed her against his body and his lips had claimed hers with untamed passion. No woman would ever tame Thanos, she brooded. Beneath his veneer of urbane sophistication she sensed power and ruthless ambition, a magnetism that commanded the respect of other men and drew beautiful women to him in droves—yet none would own him or control him, and only the most foolish would try.

The expression on his coldly handsome face was not encouraging, but she had spent the evening listening to her mother's excited chatter about her plans for the garden at Carlton House while her father had looked increasingly strained and haunted. She had finally accepted that she would do whatever it took to prevent her parents from losing their home.

Her mouth felt dry. She licked her lips nervously and prayed that when she spoke her voice would not waver. She did not want him to know how much this was costing her. 'I've come to tell you that I accept your offer,' she said baldly, lifting her head and meeting his midnight gaze steadily. 'I'll sleep with you in return for you buying Reynolds Gems, for the price my father stipulated to Vantage Investments.'

CHAPTER FOUR

FOR several long, agonising seconds Thanos said nothing, but then his brows rose and he drawled mockingly, 'I will expect you to do rather more than *sleep* in return for paying a fortune for your family's failing company.'

His body had reacted predictably to the knowledge that Tahlia was his for the taking; his arousal had been instant and uncomfortably hard. But inexplicably he'd also felt a surge of savage disappointment. When she had rejected his offer earlier that day he'd felt a grudging sense of admiration for her, but now he felt nothing but contempt. She was prepared to sell her body to protect her financial security. She was a gold-digger. He would have no compunction about taking her to bed and sating his inconvenient desire for her.

He dropped his gaze to the low-cut neckline of her dress and the provocative thrust of her breasts. *Theos,* she was beautiful. Heat surged through him and he ruthlessly ignored the faint whisper of regret that it had to be like this, that making love to her would be nothing more than a business transaction. What else could it be? he brooded. He wanted her; she wanted him to bail out her father. It was as simple and clinical as that.

Tahlia caught her breath when Thanos reached out and removed the diamanté clip that secured her chignon. Her hair fell down around her shoulders as soft as silk against her skin, and she watched his eyes darken as he wound a few pale red-gold strands around his fingers. He stayed like that for timeless seconds, his dark eyes scorching her, and then she gasped when his strong arms suddenly closed around her and he jerked her hard against his chest, his dark head swooping and his mouth claiming hers in a kiss of pure possession.

His dominance was absolute as he forced her head back on her slender neck and kissed her fiercely, demanding her complete compliance and proving beyond doubt his mastery. Instinct warned her that Thanos would be a skilled and highly experienced lover, but he had no idea that she was a novice—a virgin who had no real idea of how to please a man.

The hard ridge of his arousal nudging insistently against her thigh was proof that he wanted her, and his low growl of satisfaction when he slid his tongue deep into her mouth filled her with a mixture of apprehension and feminine triumph that she could have such an affect on him. Her senses were swamped by the subtle scent of his aftershave, and fire licked through her veins when she placed her hands on his chest and traced the bunched muscles beneath his shirt. He was so intensely, intoxicatingly male, and he aroused feelings inside her that no other man had ever made her feel.

But the voice of caution in her head, which she had ignored during the taxi ride to his hotel, was demanding to be heard.

This had gone way too far. She should never have started it in the first place, she thought frantically when he finally broke the kiss and drew back a fraction to stare down at her, his eyes glittering with sexual hunger. She ran her tongue over her lips; swollen and sensitive from the unsparing pressure of his mouth, and felt a lightning flare of reaction at her mental image of him making love to her. Her decision to offer herself to him had been born of a desperate desire to help her father.

But to sell herself to a man who despised her, who made no effort to disguise his contempt of her? That was beyond desperation—it was insane.

She opened her mouth to tell him she had made a horrendous mistake. But as she was about to utter the words a picture flashed into her mind of her mother as she had been a few months ago, painfully thin and fragile, with a silk scarf wrapped around her head to disguise the fact that she had lost her hair after numerous bouts of chemotherapy. Tonight, Vivienne had still looked fragile, but her head was now covered in baby-fine curls and her smile had been that of a woman who had cheated death and was looking forward to the rest of her life. Her parents had suffered enough, Tahlia thought fiercely. She could not sit back and allow them to lose their home.

'You don't come cheap, Tahlia,' Thanos murmured, with a deliberate inflexion on the word *cheap* that brought a flush of colour to her cheeks. 'Before I agree to pay such a substantial sum for Reynolds Gems, I think it only fair that I should see what I'm getting for my money.'

'I don't understand,' she faltered, snatching a sharp breath when he hooked his finger beneath the shoulder strap of her dress and drew it down her arm.

'I think you do,' he said softly. 'Your dress is charming, but I want to see what is beneath the pretty packaging. Take it off,' he ordered, when she remained rigidly unmoving.

End this now, the sensible voice in Tahlia's head urged frantically. *Tell him you've changed your mind, and get out of here fast.*

And then what? demanded the reckless voice inside her that she had not known existed until tonight. Go back to her parents and watch her father's emotional devastation as he broke the news to her mother that they would have to leave Carlton House?

She stared wildly at the door while her mind engaged in a fierce debate. Go—or stay, and sell her soul to the devil?

'How can I be certain that you will buy Reynolds Gems?' she asked Thanos shakily. 'I need some sort of assurance.'

'My word is the only assurance I'm prepared to give.' Thanos's eyes narrowed when she opened her mouth to argue. 'Take it—or leave it,' he shrugged uninterestedly. 'We can call the deal off.'

Tahlia's brain was racing. She had no option but to take him at his word. He was calling the shots. One night in his bed would mean that her parents' retirement would be free from financial worries. They need not know what she had done to secure their future. No one would know apart from her. And faced with the choice of sacrificing her self-respect or ensuring her parents' happiness there was no contest.

Without giving herself time to reconsider, she reached behind her and slowly slid the zip of her dress down her spine. She shot him a lightning glance, and her stomach dipped when she found him watching her intently, the expression in his dark eyes unfathomable. Don't think. Just get it over with, she told herself. And, taking a deep breath, she drew the straps of her dress down, revealing inch by inch the silver-grey strapless bra she was wearing beneath. She prayed he could not see that her hands were shaking. For this one night she must play the part of seductive temptress.

Her silk dress whispered against her skin as she drew it down over her stomach and hips and allowed the material to slither down her thighs and pool around her ankles. Her French knickers matched her bra, and her stockings were gossamer fine, topped with a wide band of lace which secured them around her slender thighs. She stepped carefully over her dress, terrified that she would stumble on her four-inch stiletto heels. She could not bring herself to look at him, but he slid his hand beneath her chin and tilted her face to his. The sultry gleam in his eyes filled her with trepidation, and at the same time a fierce jolt of shameful excitement.

She was exquisite, Thanos acknowledged, his heart kicking in his chest. He hated himself for his reaction to her, for the urgent tide of desire that swept through his body that weakened and unmanned him. He knew Tahlia possessed the morals of a whore, and he knew the pain she had caused his sister, but his awareness of her consumed him and overrode every other consideration but his need to make love to her.

He inhaled sharply, re-imposing control over his hormones, and trailed his eyes over her in a cool assessment.

'Very nice,' he drawled, watching in fascination as twin spots of colour flared on her pale cheeks. Her ability to blush at will was a useful trick in her armoury, as was her air of innocence, he reminded himself impatiently. But he could not prevent himself from reaching out and tracing the fragile line of her collarbone. Her skin felt like satin beneath his fingertips, and her long pale amber hair fell in a curtain of silk around her shoulders. He brushed it aside to reveal the slender column of her throat, then lowered his mouth to the pulse beating frenetically at its base. She smelled divine, her light floral perfume tantalising his senses and driving every thought from his head other than his burning need to possess her.

Tahlia held her breath when Thanos trailed his lips along her jaw in a feather-light caress that sent a tremor through her. Was he going to make love to her right now? Remove her bra and knickers and stroke his strong hands over her naked body before tugging her down onto the sofa? His mouth was tantalisingly close, and the gleam in his eyes filled her with apprehension—and at the same time a wild and uncontrollable excitement. There was no point in kidding herself; she wanted him to kiss her. She snatched a frantic little breath as he slowly lowered his head.

He claimed her mouth in a kiss of determined intent, forcing her lips apart and thrusting his tongue between them to explore her with erotic thoroughness. To her shame, Tahlia was lost from the first touch; he was so big and powerful, and she knew that if she fought him she would lose. Besides, she did not *want* to fight him, she acknowledged with searing honesty. Heat was coursing through her veins, and she felt boneless and supremely conscious of the melting warmth pooling between her thighs.

He increased the pressure of his mouth and slid one hand into her hair, while the other roamed up and down her body, skimmed her hips and slender waist, then curled around one breast. The brush of his thumb pad over her nipple caused it to harden beneath her sheer lace bra.

She had not expected the firestorm of emotions that raged through her. Her whole body seemed to be burning up, and the throbbing hardness of Thanos's arousal thrusting into her pelvis turned the fire into a raging inferno. She slid her hands over his chest, feeling the heat of his body through his silk shirt, and suddenly it was not enough. She wanted to feel his bare flesh beneath her fingertips. Fingers shaking slightly, she began to unfasten his buttons, revealing olive-gold skin covered with fine dark hairs, but before she had reached halfway down his abdomen he lifted his head, and his hands closed over hers in a vice like grip.

'Your eagerness to share my bed is flattering,' he drawled, watching dispassionately as colour surged into Tahlia's cheeks. 'But we have an early start in the morning, and I prefer to wait and enjoy you at my leisure.'

He had known from the moment he had taken her in his arms that one night would not be enough to pacify the ravenous beast that had taken charge of his body, Thanos acknowledged. His desire for her was beyond anything he had experienced with any other woman, and he would not be satisfied with a hurried sex session—a few snatched hours of pleasure before he left for an urgent business meeting tomorrow. For reasons he could not fathom Tahlia was a drug in his veins, and he intended to make her his mistress for as long as it took to slake his hunger for her.

'*We* have an early start?' Tahlia mumbled, so excruciatingly embarrassed by her ardent response to him and his cool rejection of her that she wanted to crawl away and die. 'I don't understand.' Had he changed his mind about wanting her? Sick fear surged through her. Had he ordered her to take off her dress because it had amused him to tease her before he revealed that he would not buy Reynolds Gems?

'It's quite simple,' he told her, picking up her dress and handing it to her. His harsh, 'Cover yourself,' brought another flare of scorching colour to her cheeks. 'I'm flying to the Greek island of Mykonos to visit my new hotel first thing in the morning—and you're coming with me. I shall require your services for one month,' he continued smoothly, ignoring Tahlia's gasp of shock. 'That should satisfy my more basic urges. I've no doubt I'll have grown bored of you after you've shared my bed for a few weeks.'

'I'm not going anywhere with you and—and certainly not for a month,' Tahlia stammered when she finally found her voice. She wobbled precariously on her high heels as she stepped into her dress and tugged it up over her hips, with scant regard for the fragile material. She thrust her arms through the straps, gasping when Thanos spun her round and slid the zip up the length of her spine.

He swung her back to face him and cupped her chin in his hand, forcing her to meet his sardonic gaze. 'You are exceptionally lovely, Tahlia, but even *you* must admit that a six-figure sum for one night of sex with you would be an extravagance—even for a billionaire.'

She blanched at the flare of contempt in his eyes, and accepted that she had taken leave of her sanity when she had agreed to sell herself to him. 'I have responsibilities here—commitments, a job…' Although she would not have one for much longer if Thanos bought out Reynolds Gems, she acknowledged dismally. The future was frighteningly uncertain. 'I can't spend a month in Greece with you,' she said dully. 'It's impossible.'

Thanos shrugged and withdrew his mobile phone from his trouser pocket. 'That's a pity, because I was just about to call Steven Holt and instruct him to proceed with buying Reynolds Gems. But if you've changed your mind I'll tell him not to go ahead.'

She was halfway across the room, heading for the door. But his words stopped her in her tracks. She turned slowly back to face him, her brain whirling. 'You can't phone him now—it's almost midnight,' she pointed out.

'I can do whatever I like,' he informed her, with a supreme arrogance that took her breath away. 'I did not make my fortune by working nine till five. My employees know that I expect them to be available whenever I need them.'

Presumably he would have the same expectation of her if she went to Greece with him? A tremor ran down Tahlia's spine at the thought. She could carry on walking out of the door and out of Thanos's life—and all her instincts were screaming at her that she *should* walk away—but he was offering her the chance to save Carlton House from repossession, the voice in her head argued. The price was high. Could she survive a month as Thanos's mistress? What was one month compared to the rest of her parents' lives?

She snatched a breath and squared her shoulders as she met his hooded gaze. 'I want written assurance that you will honour our deal. I'm afraid I don't trust your word.'

Anger surged through Thanos at her disdainful tone, but he refrained from pointing out that she was not in a position to demand anything. 'My legal team will take care of it,' he told her dismissively. 'Would you like your duties to be listed—how many times a night I will expect you to pleasure me, perhaps a description of positions…?'

'That won't be necessary,' Tahlia said sharply, conscious that her face was burning hotter than a furnace. 'I just want to be sure my father's financial worries will be over.'

'How very altruistic of you,' he murmured sardonically.

She frowned. 'What's that supposed to mean?'

He crossed to the door and held it open. 'Don't waste your breath trying to convince me that your desire to save Reynolds Gems from bankruptcy is to help your father. You have expensive tastes,' he drawled, sliding his finger over the diamanté strap of her dress and then trailing an insolent path down to her cleavage. 'Your sole interest is in ensuring your own financial security—isn't it, Tahlia?' He paused, his eyes narrowing as he glimpsed the sudden shimmer of her tears, and for a second something tugged at his insides at the knowledge that he had hurt her. He dismissed the thought ruthlessly. She deserved to be hurt—just as she had hurt Melina. 'I'll drive you home,' he said brusquely, standing aside for her to precede him out of his suite. 'You need to pack.'

There was simply no point in arguing with him, Tahlia accepted miserably as she followed him into the lift. Thanos had judged her, and he was so pig-headed that nothing she did or said would change his opinion of her. But she had glimpsed the flare of feral hunger in his eyes before his lashes swept down and hid his expression. He desired her, and he had agreed to buy Reynolds Gems in order to have her in his bed for one month. She could only pray that she would not spend the rest of her life regretting her decision to become his mistress.

After giving Thanos stilted directions to her flat Tahlia lapsed into silence, and he seemed to be lost in his own thoughts.

'I'll pick you up at eight o'clock tomorrow morning,' he told her as he parked outside her flat. 'Don't keep me waiting. And Tahlia?' he called, when she flung open the car door and hurried up her front path. 'Remember the reason why you're accompanying me on this trip and pack accordingly, won't you? I'm already fantasising about seeing you in sexy underwear like the tantalising wisps of lace you're wearing tonight.'

Face flaming, she bit back a retort which would have singed his ears and stepped into her flat, slamming the front door behind her and sagging against it. What *had* she done? she thought despairingly, burying her face in her hands as the enormity of the deal she had struck with Thanos sunk in. She had saved her parents from the devastation of losing their home, she reminded herself grimly. And with that thought in mind she dug out a suitcase from the cupboard under the stairs, pulled open her wardrobe and began to sort through its meagre contents for outfits suitable to take to Greece.

'Are you ready?' Thanos demanded curtly, when she opened the door to him at one minute past eight the following morning.

'Almost,' she muttered, annoyed that her heart immediately began to race at the sight of him, in a lightweight stone-coloured jacket and trousers, teamed with a cream shirt which was open at the throat so that she could see a tantalising V of bronzed skin. His black hair gleamed like jet in the early morning sunshine, and his beautifully sculpted features and sensual mouth caused a peculiar dragging sensation in the pit of Tahlia's stomach. 'Unfortunately Charlie is proving rather stubborn to persuade out of my bedroom.'

Black eyebrows winged skywards. 'Spare me the details of your tangled love-life,' he drawled, in the sardonic tone she detested.

'Charlie is my cat,' Tahlia informed him tightly. 'He's actually the laziest cat on the planet, and spends most of his time sleeping on my bed.' She noted Thanos's impatient frown and chewed on her bottom lip. 'You'll have to help me get him into the cat-carrier.'

She disappeared through a door and Thanos followed, glancing curiously around her bedroom. He had expected something more…seductive, he mused. The soft lemon walls, pale carpet and floral curtains and bedspread were fresh and pretty, but he could not imagine her entertaining a stream of lovers here.

A hissing sound like a kettle coming to the boil came from under the dresser, and he stared in surprise at the fat ginger cat whose yellow eyes were fixed menacingly on him. Tahlia was on her knees, dangling a rubber toy in front of the cat to tempt it into the carrier.

'Come on, Charlie,' she crooned. 'Come and play.' The hissing grew louder, and the cat suddenly sprang, hooking its claws in Tahlia's hand. 'Quick—grab him!' she yelled.

'You must be joking.' Instead Thanos manoeuvred the carrier over the cat, and after a brief tussle Tahlia managed to deposit the ball of orange fur inside and hastily secured the door. Blood was running down her hand and the cat was still spitting furiously. '*Theos,*' he muttered. 'What breed is it—a wild cat?'

'He's just a bit sensitive,' Tahlia told him seriously. 'I got him from the cat rescue centre, and I think he was badly treated by his previous owners. He's a sweetie, really.'

'I'll take your word for it. You'd better put some antiseptic on that scratch.' Thanos frowned. Giving a home to a stray cat with homicidal tendencies did not fit in with his image of Tahlia, he brooded irritably. He picked up her suitcase and cast another look around her room, pausing at the photograph on the bedside table. 'Is this your brother?' he asked curiously, as he studied the picture of Tahlia and a tall man with bright red hair.

'No, I don't have any siblings.' She slipped on her jacket and flicked her hair back from her face. 'That's Michael. We met on my first day at university, when he told me that redheads should always stick together.' She smiled softly at the memory. 'Michael was studying to be a vet, but he died of meningitis a few months before he graduated.'

Thanos heard the sudden huskiness in her voice. 'Was he your boyfriend?' he queried abruptly, irritated with himself for his curiosity. Tahlia's personal life had nothing to do with him.

She shrugged. 'We'd been dating for a few months.' Over the years she had come to terms with losing Michael, but only her closest friends knew how devastated she had been by his death. She had no intention of confiding in Thanos. She picked up the cat-carrier and glanced at him. 'I'm ready to leave now.'

Tahlia's tone warned Thanos that she did not want to continue the conversation, and he was suddenly impatient to leave. He did not want to hear that she had suffered a tragedy in her past. For the past six months he had envisaged her as a cold-hearted bitch, and he refused to contemplate any possibility that he might have been wrong.

'I hope you're not planning to try and smuggle that cat through Customs?' he said tersely as they walked out to the car.

'Of course not. Hobson is going to look after him. He used to be my parents' butler, but he's semi-retired now, and lives in an annexe of Carlton House,' Tahlia explained. 'We'll have to take Charlie over to him.'

'Is the house on the way to Gatwick?'

'The opposite direction, I'm afraid. But I can't leave Charlie to fend for himself. I guess it's a case of love me, love my cat,' she quipped, as Thanos deposited the cat carrier on the back seat and opened the front passenger door for her.

'Hell will freeze over before I do either,' Thanos said violently.

He fired the ignition and pulled away from the kerb, but his scathing comment hung in the air between them, and Tahlia quickly turned her head and stared out of the window, wondering why her eyes were stinging with stupid tears. Thanos could not make it plainer that he hated her, but she was shocked at how much his contempt hurt.

She said nothing more, apart from giving him directions to Carlton House, and only glanced at him when he drove through the gates and gave a low whistle.

'I see why your parents are so keen to hang on to the house,' he said dryly, as he stared up at the ivy-covered walls and the three storeys of mullioned windows glinting in the sunlight. 'It's spectacular.'

'For many generations it was passed down to the oldest son of the family, but my mother was an only child so she inherited it,' Tahlia explained. 'It's a Grade I listed building, and to be honest the cost of its upkeep is a nightmare. My parents do their best to maintain it, even though it's a drain on their resources, and Mum is very proud of her heritage. She loves Carlton House. It would break her heart to leave it—'

She broke off, blushing at the knowledge that she had agreed to become Thanos's mistress to keep Carlton House safe. The front door of the house suddenly swung open, and an elderly, impeccably dressed man walked slowly down the front steps.

'Who is that?'

'That's Hobson.'

Thanos frowned. 'He can't still work for your parents, surely? He must be ninety.'

'We think he's in his late seventies, although he won't actually admit his true age,' Tahlia explained as she climbed out of the car and took the cat-carrier from the back seat. 'He started working here as a butler for my grandparents; my parents feel that Carlton is as much his house as it is theirs. My father has promised Hobson that he will always have a home here.' Her smile faded as the implication of her words struck her. If Carlton was repossessed, where would Hobson go? He had no family, and he would be as distraught as her parents if he had to leave the house that had been his home for fifty years.

It wasn't going to happen, she reassured herself as she walked up the drive to greet the butler. Thanos had promised to buy Reynolds Gems, Carlton would be safe, and she would take the secret that she had sold herself to him to her grave.

'I was wondering how you had booked me onto a flight at such short notice,' Tahlia murmured an hour later, as she followed Thanos across the tarmac at Gatwick airport. 'I suppose I should have guessed you own a plane.'

'I travel extensively for my business, and the Lear jet is more convenient than relying on scheduled flights,' he replied, his eyes narrowing on her faintly stunned expression as she followed him onto the plane. His lip curled into a sardonic grimace as he watched her glance around at the plush leather seats. Women were always impressed by the jet, and several of his ex-lovers had been eager to join the mile-high club. He could spend the flight to Greece enjoying Tahlia's gorgeous body in the luxurious bedroom at the far end of the plane— she was hardly likely to object, he mused cynically. She had made it clear she would do whatever pleased him in return for him shelling out a lot of money for Reynolds Gems.

He could not deny he was tempted, he thought irritably, and he skimmed his eyes over her, from her silky red-gold hair—worn loose today, and falling in a smooth sheet down her back—to her elegant cream skirt and jacket teamed with a sapphire-coloured blouse which matched the startling blue of her eyes, finally to her shapely legs sheathed in fine hose, their slender length emphasised by her three-inch stiletto heels. She looked cool and classy, and he felt a violent urge to lower his head and kiss her until her lips were no longer coated in a pale gloss but were red and swollen, as she parted them invitingly beneath his, as she had done in his hotel suite the previous night. Beneath her haughty façade this aristocratic English rose was hot, and she had already shown her willingness to explore the sexual chemistry that simmered between them. But he wanted to enjoy her at his leisure. He would have to curb his impatience until they reached Greece.

Four hours later, Tahlia stared out of the window as the plane swooped low over a cobalt-blue sea sparkling beneath a cloudless sky, dotted with several emerald islands. 'I hadn't expected the land to be so green,' she murmured, her spirits lifting as she absorbed the spectacular view of the Cyclades Islands.

'That's Mykonos just ahead of us.' Thanos's deep voice sounded close to her ear, and she jerked her head around to find that he had closed his laptop, which he had been working on for the entire flight. 'The smaller island closest to it is Delos. It is uninhabited, but it's one of the most important archaeological sites in Greece, and is believed in Greek mythology to be the birthplace of the goddess Artemis—hence the name of my new hotel,' he added with a faint smile.

Tahlia's eyes were drawn to the sensual curve of his mouth

and her heart flipped. She had been agonisingly conscious of him during the flight, but as soon as the jet had taken off he had become absorbed in his work and not spared her a word or glance. He had not brought her to Greece for her conversational skills, she reminded herself heavily. Her sole duty for the next month was to please him in bed—but considering her lack of experience in that department she feared he was going to be disappointed.

The Artemis Hotel was situated a few kilometres from Mykonos Town, at the charming beach resort of Agios Ioannis. The vast white-walled, flat-roofed building was impressive, and the reception area no less so, with its pale marble floors and pillars teamed with beautiful leather sofas and chairs in muted shades of blue and grey.

'The whole place is stunning,' Tahlia commented when Thanos had given her a lightning tour of the four dining rooms, six bars and the spa and leisure complex.

'I'm pleased with it,' he replied as he led the way along a velvet-carpeted corridor. The walls were hung with numerous works of art, many of them contemporary pieces, and Tahlia wondered if Thanos had bought any of Rufus Hartman's paintings from the art exhibition where they had first met. She grimaced. Was it really only a few days ago? It felt like a lifetime.

'This is my private suite,' he explained as he halted at the end of the corridor and flung open a door.

Tahlia followed him into an airy sitting room, her heart suddenly beating too fast as she glanced through a door to her right and glimpsed a king-sized bed. She wondered if Thanos expected her to begin her duties as his mistress immediately, but he had walked over to the long wall of windows and opened the French doors leading to the terrace. She followed him, and caught her breath at the uninterrupted view of the crystalline sea and an aquamarine swimming pool below them.

'The suite has its own pool,' he explained, indicating the rectangular pool to one side of the terrace. 'The main pool you can see below us is actually a salt-water pool, separated from the sea by a terraced area where guests can sunbathe and enjoy the view of the bay.'

'It's beautiful,' Tahlia murmured as she stared down at the hotel's pool, which had been cleverly designed so that it appeared to spill into the sea beyond. She lifted her face to the sun, her hair rippling in the warm Aegean breeze.

Thanos resisted the urge to wind the silky strands around his hand, pull her in and capture her mouth in a hungry kiss that he knew instinctively could only end when he swept her into his arms and carried her through to the bedroom. She unsettled him more than he cared to admit, and he found his reaction to her intensely irritating. Even forcing himself to think of Melina—now staying at a rehabilitation clinic in the US, where she was slowly learning to walk again—did not diminish his awareness of the woman at his side.

Had his father struggled to control his attraction to the English tart Wendy Jones, who had become his mistress? he brooded. For the first time in his life he understood the guilt associated with wanting a woman when it was morally wrong to desire her.

He swung round abruptly and walked back across the terrace. 'You have the rest of the day to enjoy the view. I have a meeting scheduled with my management team, which I imagine will last for several hours.'

Tahlia frowned, unsure of exactly what her role in his life was to be. 'What do you expect me to do while you're gone?' she asked as she followed him back inside.

He shrugged dismissively. 'Whatever you like. You can swim, or read—all the rooms at the Artemis have a selection of current magazines. And of course you will need to prepare for tonight.'

Tahlia's mouth suddenly felt dry at the prospect of the night ahead. In what way did he expect her to prepare? Did the Artemis also leave copies of the *Kama Sutra* in the rooms, for guests to flick through? she wondered, panic churning in the pit of her stomach.

Thanos's eyes narrowed on the hectic flush staining her cheeks. 'Tonight we're dining with the mayor of Mykonos and other council dignitaries. You'll need to dress up.' He gave her a mocking smile. 'Wear something sexy, hmm…? After all, the sole reason you are here is to please me.' He gathered up his briefcase, but instead of heading for the door he walked towards her, his mouth curving into an amused smile that was not reflected in his cold eyes. 'You can start by pleasing me now,' he said coolly, and he cupped her chin in his hand and bent his head, bringing his mouth down on hers before she had a chance to pull away.

The kiss was hard, almost brutal, a statement of possession and a warning of intent that tonight he would demand so much more. Tahlia wanted to deny him, wanted to firm her lips against his probing tongue, but to her shame the moment he touched her she was lost, swept up in the fire that consumed them both. She had been acutely aware of him ever since he had picked her up from her flat that morning, and now her senses were set alight by the scent of his cologne and another, totally masculine scent that belonged to this man alone.

He caught her despairing sigh and ruthlessly took advantage of her parted lips to thrust his tongue between them, exploring the moist warmth of her mouth until she was boneless and clung to him, sliding her hands to his shoulders and running her fingers through the thick dark hair that curled at his nape.

He was breathing hard when he finally released her, and Tahlia took a tiny shard of comfort in the fact that he could not hide the evidence that he was affected by the wild passion they shared.

'I'll see you later,' he said tersely, stepping away from her, but she had the impression that his control was balanced on a knife-edge, and that if she gave any indication that she wanted him to stay he would seize her in his arms once more and kiss her until kissing was not enough for either of them.

She remained silent, shocked and ashamed by her reaction to him, and with a curt nod he strode from the room. Only then did she release her breath. It was crazy and utterly inexplicable, she thought shakily as she held her fingers against her swollen mouth. Thanos believed he had good reason to despise her, and she was well aware that his one aim was to punish her. Yet neither of them, it seemed, could control the wildfire sexual attraction which blazed between them.

CHAPTER FIVE

THERE was no sign of Tahlia when Thanos walked into his private suite that evening, but it was late, and he assumed that she was getting changed for dinner. His meeting had overrun by several long and frustrating hours, and the discovery that preparations for the party to celebrate the official opening of the Artemis were way behind schedule had put him in a foul mood. He needed to have been in Greece these past few months, to oversee the completion of the new hotel, but thanks to Tahlia and his sleazeball ex-brother-in-law he had been at Melina's hospital bedside in the States instead of running his company.

He crossed to the bar and poured himself a large Scotch, added ice to the glass and took a long sip as he strolled onto the terrace. Dusk had fallen, painting the sky in hues of purple and indigo, and the first stars glimmered as brightly as the lights of the tavernas and hotels that delineated the coast. But the peaceful scene did nothing to lift his mood, and when a faint noise from behind him alerted him to Tahlia's presence he swung round, his brows lowering in a slashing frown as he studied her.

'What made you think that dressing like a nun would please me?' he queried, in a dangerously soft tone. He noted her mutinous expression and his mouth curled into a hard smile. 'Or did you deliberately choose your most unattractive outfit to flout me?'

His guess was not too far from the truth, and Tahlia blushed. At the same time she felt a spurt of annoyance at his description of her as unattractive. It was true her faithful black skirt was years old and unfashionably long, and her cream silk-organza blouse with its high neck and a row of tiny pearl buttons running down the front could in no way be called sexy. But she had swept her hair up into an elegant chignon and taken care with her make-up. She didn't think she looked a complete frump. Thanos, however, clearly held a different opinion.

'I'm not taking you to dinner when you look like my maiden aunt,' he said tersely. 'Go and get changed while I shower, and be ready to leave in fifteen minutes.' His brows rose when she did not move. 'Of course I could always strip you myself—but if that happens I can guarantee we will miss dinner altogether.'

Tahlia flushed at the hungry gleam in his eyes. 'You can't tell me what to do. You don't own me,' she said angrily, frantically trying to banish the image of Thanos removing her clothes and then his, and the even more shocking idea of them showering together.

His mocking smile told her he had read her mind, and her insides squirmed in embarrassment. 'For the next month I can do exactly what I like with you,' he warned her, in a voice laced with such blatant sexual intent that a shiver ran the length of her spine. His patience suddenly evaporated, and he caught hold of her hand and marched her across the lounge to the bedroom. 'I'll find you something suitable to wear,' he growled, but his frown deepened when he flung open the wardrobe and flicked through the few outfits she had brought with her.

'Why did you bring so little with you when you knew you were coming to Greece for a month?' His eyes narrowed. 'Or did you hope I would grow bored of you sooner?' He reached out and tugged the clip from her carefully arranged chignon, so that her hair tumbled around her shoulders. The sultry gleam in his dark gaze sent a tremor through Tahlia's body as stark awareness uncoiled in the pit of her stomach. 'If so, then I fear you will be disappointed,' he murmured, lowering his head so that his breath fanned her lips. 'The sexual chemistry between us is at combustion point, my beautiful English rose, and I am seriously beginning to doubt that one month will satisfy my desire for you.'

His mouth was so close to hers that Tahlia shut her eyes, certain that he was about to kiss her. The exotic scent of his cologne swamped her senses, and there was no thought in her head to resist him. But to her shock he suddenly moved away from her. Startled, she let her lashes fly open, and she found that she was standing with her mouth still parted in readiness for his kiss. The sound of his soft, mocking laughter filled her with mortification at the shameful sense of longing that he would snatch her into his arms and ravage her mouth with primitive passion.

Thanos closed the wardrobe with a decisive snap. 'There is nothing in there that excites me,' he said bluntly. 'You will have to stay as you are tonight, but tomorrow you will go shopping. We'll be attending many social events while we are here and you'll need several evening dresses, as well as daywear.'

Tahlia thought of her latest credit card bill, which she had no means of paying off, and shook her head. 'I can't afford to buy new clothes,' she admitted wearily, her temper flaring at Thanos's sardonic expression. He believed she led the life of a pampered princess, but nothing could be further from the truth. 'The clothes I've brought with me are all that I own. My father hasn't been able to pay my salary for the last three months. Every penny went into keeping Reynolds Gems solvent. I worked for nothing in the desperate hope that we could save the company,' she explained when he looked disbelieving. 'I sold most of my clothes, and my jewellery, but I didn't make enough to cover my bills and living expenses. I'm struggling to cover even the minimum payment on my credit cards, and a shopping spree is out of the question. You'll just have to take me as I am,' she finished defiantly, and then blushed scarlet as she realised what she had said.

'I am very much looking forward to taking you, Tahlia,' Thanos assured her gravely, the glinting amusement in his eyes masking his shock at her assertion that her life in London had *not* been one of luxury and over-indulgence, as he had assumed.

Of course she could be lying, he mused. Experience had taught him that most women were accomplished liars—none more so than Yalena, when she had been sleeping with one of his closest friends at the same time as swearing her love for him. But his gut instinct told him that Tahlia was telling the truth about her financial situation. No wonder she had agreed to be his mistress in return for him buying her father's company, he thought cynically. He knew from the numerous photos of her in the press that she liked to dress in haute couture. No doubt she would spend her share of the proceeds of the sale of Reynolds Gems on restocking her wardrobe.

He glanced at his watch, and then strolled towards the *en suite* bathroom. 'We're running seriously late, so I'll have to wait until tonight for the pleasure of taking you to bed,' he drawled. 'As for shopping—I will be paying for your clothes. Think of it as one of the perks of being my mistress,' he said in a harder tone, when she opened her mouth to argue. 'I want to see you in sexy clothes that flatter your gorgeous body. Not in an outfit that makes you look as though you are auditioning for a role in *The Sound of Music*.'

* * *

Dinner was the ordeal Tahlia had expected. In ordinary circumstances she would have enjoyed the stunning décor and
the ambience of the Artemis's gold-star restaurant, where a
celebrated French chef had prepared four superb courses. But
from the moment Thanos led her over to the table where his
guests were already seated and introduced her as his 'companion' she felt so painfully self-conscious—everyone must
have guessed she was his mistress—that she could do no
more than toy with her food.

As well as the dignitaries from Mykonos, three of Thanos's
top executives were also present, and although everyone spoke
in English rather than Greek, her attempts at conversation
with them were stilted. They clearly thought she was a bimbo,
and one of the executives, a man Thanos had introduced as
Antonis Lykaios, watched her avidly throughout the meal,
trailing his eyes over her as if he were mentally undressing her.

Tahlia was torn between longing for the evening to be over
and praying that it would last for ever—because what was to
come next was certain to be a hundred times worse, she
brooded. Her eyes were drawn to Thanos. He looked breathtaking tonight, in a black dinner suit and a white silk shirt, his
dark hair swept back from his brow and the flickering light
from the table's centrepiece of candles highlighting the sharp
edges of his cheekbones. He was urbane, sophisticated, and
no doubt a skilful lover, she thought, feeling a rush of shaming
heat flood through her when he looked across the table and
their glances locked.

The voices around her faded, and she was reminded of the
first time she had seen him at the art gallery, when she had
felt as though they were the only two people in the universe.
She watched his eyes darken with a sensual promise that
made her mouth run dry, and butterflies leapt in her stomach.
It was not Thanos she was afraid of, she acknowledged

bleakly; it was herself and her pathetic inability to resist him. It was utterly ridiculous to feel so drawn to a man who openly admitted that he despised her, but when she had first seen him at Rufus Hartman's exhibition—before she had learned that he blamed her for his sister's accident—she had felt an emotional bond with him which defied logic or common sense. A voice in her head had whispered that he was the 'the one' she had been waiting all her life to meet.

'Would you like more wine, Tahlia?' Antonis Lykaios leaned towards her, proffering a bottle of Chardonnay, and Tahlia was so grateful for the excuse to drag her eyes from Thanos that she forgot how her skin had crawled when Antonis had leered at her and smiled at him.

Across the table Thanos fought the urge to rearrange his junior executive's handsome face with his fist—before continuing the caveman tactics by throwing Tahlia over his shoulder and carrying her off to his bed. How *dared* she flirt with Lykaios in front of him? he thought furiously. But what had he expected? In recent months the British tabloids had regularly reported on her energetic love-life with Z-list celebrities. Clearly she would flirt with any man under seventy.

He gave a brief nod to his chief executive, indicating that it was time to bring the evening to an end, before his gaze strayed back to Tahlia. His initial opinion that her outfit was unflattering had been wrong, he thought irritably. At first glance she looked chaste and demure in the high-necked blouse, but look closer and it was possible to see the outline of her breasts beneath the sheer material. His fingers itched to unfasten every one of those tiny buttons and slowly reveal her delectable body. With her pale red-gold hair falling in a silky curtain around her shoulders and a subtle pink gloss on her lips she looked incredibly sexy, and he was infuriated by the knowledge that he was not the only man at the dinner table who could not keep his eyes off her.

The dinner party eventually came to an end, and Tahlia stifled a sigh of relief when the guests stood up from the table. Antonis Lykaios seemed to have taken her smile as a sign that she was interested in him; twice she had had to forcibly remove his hand from her thigh beneath the table-cloth, and she forced herself not to flinch now, when he lifted her fingers to his mouth and kissed them in a theatrical farewell gesture. She saw Thanos's brows lower in a slashing frown, and her sense of foreboding escalated when they crossed the marble vestibule to the lift and he surveyed her in a brooding silence as they travelled to the top floor.

'I realise that you automatically flirt with anyone in trousers,' he drawled as followed her into his suite, discarding his jacket and tie and flinging them carelessly over the back of a chair. 'But Antonis Lykaios is engaged, and I will not allow you to sink your predatory claws into him.'

'I pity his fiancée,' she snapped, her temper flaring at the undisguised contempt in his voice. 'Your executive was flirting with *me*, and I'd be grateful if you would tell him to keep his sweaty hands to himself in future.' She closed her eyes against the pain stabbing at her skull, aware that her headache was due as much to the two glasses of wine she had drunk although she had eaten very little dinner, as to her rising nervous tension. Thanos was heart-stoppingly sexy, with his dark hair falling onto his brow, but he also looked grim and forbidding, and the prospect of giving her virginity to him when he had made it plain that he despised her was suddenly unendurable.

She lifted a hand to massage her temples, and pleaded shakily, 'Thanos, can we talk?'

His dark brows lifted in an expression of arrogant amusement. 'Talking is the last thing I have in mind for tonight.' He strolled towards her and drew her hand away from her face. 'We made a deal, Tahlia,' he reminded her, his voice suddenly harsh and his eyes glittering with cold indifference. 'And now the time has come for you to honour your side of it.'

Her heart was thudding so hard that it hurt to breathe. 'Please…' she cried urgently. 'I swear I had no idea that James was married to your sister…'

She was prevented from saying any more when Thanos placed his finger across her lips. 'Save your lies—and your tears.' He surveyed her over-bright eyes dispassionately, and brushed away the single tear that slipped down her cheek with his thumb. 'I'm not taken in by either,' he said savagely, and lowered his head, capturing her mouth in a punishing kiss that sought to dominate as he forced her lips apart with a bold flick of his tongue.

Once again he had moved with the speed of a panther, pouncing for the kill, and once again Tahlia was unprepared for the molten heat that swept through her the instant he touched her. What was wrong with her? she wondered despairingly. Pride dictated that she should remain stiff and unresponsive in Thanos's arms, but he intoxicated her senses so that she could not think logically, and she was conscious only of the slight abrasion of his cheek against hers, the tingling sensation in her breasts as he crushed her against his chest.

Thanos finally lifted his head and stared down at her, his eyes gleaming when she unconsciously traced her tongue over her swollen lips. 'This madness is not mine alone. You feel it too,' he grated, his fury and frustration palpable—and yet Tahlia sensed that his anger was directed as much at himself as her, and she knew that, like her, he was startled by the intensity of the sexual chemistry which blazed between them. 'You are like a fever in my blood,' he said hoarsely. 'I wanted you from the moment I saw you, and now I cannot wait any longer.'

'Thanos…no!' She gave a shocked cry when he moved his hands to the neck of her blouse and wrenched the fragile material apart, so that little pearl buttons pinged in all directions. Before she had time to react he reached around and unsnapped her bra, casting the delicate scrap of lace to the floor so that her small pale breasts were exposed to his heated gaze.

He was breathing hard, and Tahlia watched in fascination as dull colour flared along his magnificent cheekbones. The feral hunger in his eyes made her tremble with a mixture of apprehension and an unbidden shivery excitement. No man had ever looked at her the way Thanos was doing now, and she instinctively tried to cover her breasts with her hands.

He caught her wrists and tugged them down to her sides. 'Don't hide yourself from me,' he said harshly. 'I want to feast my eyes on every inch of your delectable body.'

His words made Tahlia tremble—not with fear, she acknowledged, but with a feverish excitement she could not deny. Her heart slammed in her chest when he pushed her hair over her shoulders, then slid his hand down her body and curled his fingers possessively over her breast. She tensed, expecting him to be rough, but his palm was warm on her bare flesh, and when he stroked his thumb-pad across her nipple in a feather-light caress she gasped as exquisite sensation arced through her.

'Not just beautiful, but delightfully responsive,' Thanos drawled.

She blushed scarlet at the undisguised satisfaction in his voice, but her body seemed to have a will of its own, and she could do nothing to prevent the dusky nipples from swelling into taut peaks. He moved his hand to her other breast and rolled the swollen nipple between his thumb and forefinger, sending another lightning bolt of sensation spiralling down to the pit of her stomach. She caught her breath when he tugged her backwards and lowered his head to the slender arch of her body.

He flicked his tongue back and forth over her nipple, building her pleasure to a level that was almost unbearable, and she gave a choked cry when he finally desisted in teasing her and clamped his mouth around the provocative peak. The sensation of him suckling her was so breathtaking that her lashes drifted down and she gave herself up to the storm he was creating, gasping with pleasure when he moved to her other breast and laved the throbbing peak with firm, wet strokes of his tongue.

She was dimly aware of Thanos dragging her skirt over her hips, and he muttered something in Greek in a hoarse tone when he eased away from her and trailed his eyes down from her pouting breasts to her flat stomach, then lower to her black lace knickers and gossamer-fine black stockings. Tahlia held her breath when he placed his hand on the strip of creamy flesh above her stocking-top, and she felt liquid heat flood between her thighs. Was he going to take her here and now? Drag her to the floor and spread her beneath him on the carpet?

Tension gripped her. Until now she had always believed that she would only ever make love when she was in a loving relationship. She had loved Michael, but their gentle romance had still been in its early stages when he had been snatched from her; she had thought she loved James, but he had lied to her, and she was glad she had discovered his treachery before they had become lovers. Maybe it was time she gave up on love, she thought bleakly. There was no love between her and Thanos. Just mistrust and dislike and a searing passion that obliterated every logical thought and demanded to be appeased. She had agreed to have sex with him in return for her parents' financial security and she would not back out now. But it was only fair that she tell him she was not the experienced seductress he believed.

Thanos stared down at Tahlia's semi-naked body and drew a ragged breath, his nostrils flaring as he fought to bring his raging hormones under control. The delicate skin of her inner thigh felt like satin beneath his fingers, and the urge to move his hand higher and slip it beneath her lacy knickers was so strong that it took every ounce of his formidable will-power to deny himself the pleasure of touching her intimately. His brain acknowledged what she had done—how she had hurt Melina—but his body did not seem to care that she that she was an immoral slut, and it was on fire for her.

'Thanos… I have to tell you…' Her voice shook, but he ruthlessly hardened his heart against her.

'But I don't have to listen—and certainly not to more of your lies and excuses,' he said harshly, disregarding her startled cry as he swept her up into his arms and strode towards the bedroom.

Tahlia was shaking so badly she was sure Thanos must feel the tremors running through her body. Perhaps he thought she was trembling with excitement? She could not bear to meet his gaze and see his familiar mocking expression, so instead she curled her arms around his neck, pressing her face against his shoulder while he carried her. It was not too late to stop this, a voice whispered in her head. She could tell Thanos she would rather sell her soul to the devil than trade her body for hard cash. But what about her parents? another voice screamed inside her. How could she allow them to lose their home and the worry-free retirement they deserved?

Thanos shouldered open the door of the master bedroom, strode over to the bed, and laid Tahlia down on the peacock-blue satin bedspread. Her glorious hair fanned across the pillows in a halo of shimmering gold. He could not resist winding a long silky strand around his fingers, and heat surged through him as he lowered his eyes to her breasts and feasted on their milky-pale beauty.

Why Tahlia? he asked himself angrily. He had never wanted any woman the way he wanted her. His desire was mindless, desperate, an irresistible force clamouring to be assuaged, and his body shook with need as he stretched out beside her and pressed his mouth to the fragile line of her collarbone. She tasted of ambrosia, her skin as soft as rose petals beneath his lips, and he could not resist tracing them down her body, pausing at each breast to anoint its blush-pink tip, relishing the feel of her nipples swelling inside his mouth before he moved lower still.

Her sweetly puckered navel invited him to explore it with his tongue. He felt the tremor that ran through her, but she made no effort to touch him, and lay passive while he caressed her, as if she were somehow detached from her surroundings— from him. Anger coiled inside him. Did she think she could simply lie there, as unresponsive as a marble figurine while he took his pleasure? When he had finished with her would she wash herself clean of his touch? Believing that the price she had paid for her parents' house had been worth soiling herself for? He did not want a sacrificial offering, he thought grimly. He wanted her warm and willing in his bed, and he was determined that soon she would be begging for his possession.

Tahlia stiffened when she felt Thanos's hand slip between her thighs. Until the moment he had laid her on his bed she had been cocooned in a curious sense of unreality. It seemed impossible to believe that she had actually agreed to have sex with him, that he really would make love to her. But the feel of his hands and mouth on her skin, moving ever lower down her body, had catapulted her back to reality, and now fear churned in her stomach at the prospect of giving her virginity to him.

Hysteria formed a bubble in her throat as she imagined his reaction if she asked him to be gentle. He was convinced that she had been his brother-in-law's mistress, and she could hear his scathing laughter if she told him that this was her first time. He would not believe her. And if he did—if he realised that she was innocent—he might well reject her and call off their deal. She could not risk that happening. She was going to have to put on the act of a lifetime, she thought numbly, and pretend that she was as experienced as he assumed.

His palm felt warm and faintly abrasive on the sensitive skin of her inner thigh, and she forced herself to relax as he hooked his fingers in the waistband of her knickers and slowly drew them over her hips.

'Beautiful,' he murmured, his voice thick with sexual tension. She felt his hand brush gently through the triangle of gold curls, and her heart slammed in her chest when he ran his finger lightly up and down the lips of her vagina, so that they swelled and opened like the petals of a flower, moist and sweetly scented with her arousal, ready for him to explore her. He leaned over her to claim her mouth in a slow, drugging kiss that lit a flame deep inside her and banished her fears. His lips no longer sought to dominate but were gently persuasive, decimating her resistance so that she opened her mouth beneath his and kissed him back with hungry fervour.

Her breath hitched in her throat when she felt him gently part her, and she heard his low growl of satisfaction when he discovered the slick wetness of her arousal. She felt boneless, mindless, and she allowed him to spread her legs wider, excitement cascading through her when she felt his finger probe her velvet folds and slip between them. How could it be wrong when it felt so utterly and exquisitely right? she wondered dazedly. Instinctively she arched her hips so that he could slide his finger deeper into her, and she could not hold back a moan of pleasure when he stretched her wider and inserted another finger, moving his hand with delicate skill so that she writhed with the pleasure he was creating.

'Undress me.'

The starkness of his command sent a jolt of trepidation through Tahlia, but her apprehension was mixed with irresistible sexual curiosity. His wickedly inventive fingers had aroused her to a fever pitch of desire, and she wanted… She did not know what she wanted, she acknowledged as she shifted her hips restlessly. This was all new to her. Her body felt tense and strung out, and only Thanos could soothe the dragging ache deep inside her.

She fumbled with his shirt buttons, her movements jerky and uncoordinated, but finally she spread the material aside and skimmed her hands over satin skin overlaid with crisp dark hairs. She could feel the heat emanating from him, and her senses flared as she inhaled the sensual musk of his cologne mingled with the subtle perfume of male pheromones. He dominated her mind and captivated her soul so that the world faded and nothing existed but Thanos, and the erotic glide of his hands and mouth over her trembling body.

Her lashes had drifted down, as if she could blot out the reality of what she was doing, but she was aware of him easing away from her as her skin quickly cooled, bereft of the warmth of his powerful body. She opened her eyes to discover that he had stripped down to his underwear. His black silk boxers could not disguise the jutting strength of his arousal, and when her gaze flicked upwards to his face the feral gleam in his eyes caused her heart to miss a beat. There was no going back; the message thudded in her brain, and she licked her suddenly dry lips with the tip of her tongue as he stepped out of his boxers and stood before her, his bronzed, muscle-bound body as beautiful as a work of art, his powerful erection jutting proudly forward as he strode purposefully over to the bed.

'I want you so badly I'm in danger of exploding,' Thanos said hoarsely, his Greek accent sounding very pronounced. His capacity for logical thought had deserted him and his self-control was non-existent, while his body throbbed with a level of need that he had never experienced before. Tahlia's slender, pale beauty summoned him, and the drumbeat of desire pounding in his veins overwhelmed him. 'I apologise for the lack of leisurely seduction, but I have to have you *now*. And you are ready for me, Tahlia,' he said thickly, his voice deepening with satisfaction as he slipped his hand between her thighs and discovered the drenching sweetness of her arousal.

He could not wait, and swiftly donned protection before joining her on the bed. The mattress dipped as he positioned himself over her and pushed her legs wider apart. He surged forward, rubbing the sensitive tip of his manhood against her until she opened for him. She was tighter than he had expected, and as she tensed he hesitated, confused by the sudden flare of panic in her eyes. He frowned and drew back a little, but already her muscles were stretching to accommodate him, drawing him into a velvet embrace so that he could think of nothing but thrusting into her again, deeper this time, so that he filled her with his swollen shaft.

Tahlia's muscles had clenched at the realisation that Thanos was about to join his body with hers. She had always dreamed that this moment would be special, that she would give her virginity to the man she loved. A wave of intense sadness surged up inside her, but there was no time to think or refuse him, and her eyes widened in shock as she felt the hard length of his arousal push insistently against her femininity. She had no choice but to accept him into her.

To her surprise there was no pain, just an unfamiliar feeling of fullness, and she released her breath on a shaky sigh as he drew back a little and then eased forward once more, until their bodies were locked together in the most intimate embrace of all. Thanos was part of her. She had given herself to him. In some deep and elemental way she was now his for all time, she thought wonderingly as he moved inside her, setting a rhythm that she knew instinctively would take her to somewhere wonderful but as yet remained frustratingly out of reach.

Thanos slid his hands beneath her bottom and lifted her hips, driving into her with faster, deeper strokes. There was no tenderness in his actions. This was sex at its most basic, Tahlia acknowledged, urgent and hungry, driving them both towards the edge. She was dimly aware that her breath was coming in shallow gasps, and when she opened her eyes she saw that Thanos's face was a rigid mask, the cords on his neck standing out as he drove relentlessly into her.

'Don't stop…don't stop…' She was unaware of her urgent cries, her whole being concentrated on the insistent throbbing deep in her pelvis.

Thanos snatched a harsh breath, fighting for control, but the battle had been lost from the moment he had penetrated Tahlia's body and found her tight and hot and utterly irresistible. To his utter shock he realised that he could not hold back. It had never happened to him before, this complete loss of self-control, but he could not help it. His mind and body were focused on reaching that magical place where he would experience the release he craved, and with one final savage thrust his control shattered. A primal groan of male satisfaction was wrenched from his throat as his whole body convulsed with pleasure.

For a few moments he remained slumped on top of her, his chest heaving as he dragged oxygen into his lungs. He was still stunned by what had happened, by the tidal wave that had swept through him and demolished his restraint so that he had selfishly snatched his own pleasure.

Shame seared him, and he lifted his head to stare down at her.

'I'm sorry,' he grated harshly.

'For what?' she whispered.

'Don't you know?' He frowned, puzzled by the look of genuine confusion in her eyes. It could not possibly have been her first time, he reminded himself forcefully. He had evidence that she had been James Hamilton's mistress. Her air of innocence was an illusion. Yet he could not forget her expression when he had first thrust into her, the fleeting fear in her eyes that had been replaced by a look of wonderment. Could it be that she had never experienced an orgasm with any of her previous lovers and so did not know what she had missed?

His male pride was hurt by the knowledge that he had been no better than the other men she had slept with. Driven by his overpowering need for satisfaction he had been impatient, had come before she had climaxed. He rolled off her, propped himself up on one elbow, and skimmed his hand lightly over her stomach, down to the cluster of gold curls between her legs. His mouth curved into a small smile when he felt the tremor that ran through her. His hunger for her had overwhelmed him, but now he was sated—temporarily, at least, he acknowledged wryly as his body stirred—and he knew that with patience he could bring her to the peak of ecstasy.

He lowered his head to her breast and flicked his tongue lazily across her swollen nipple, heard her sharply indrawn breath when he drew the reddened crest fully into his mouth and suckled her. She twisted her hips restlessly, and he smiled again against her skin as he moved to her other breast and meted out the same exquisite torture before trailing his lips down over her flat stomach.

'Thanos…? Tahlia murmured uncertainly when he pushed

her legs apart. The knowledge that he was looking intently at the most intimate part of her body was shockingly arousing, and the dragging sensation in her pelvis, which had eased when he had withdrawn from her, uncoiled in a sharp tug of desire. 'No!'

Too late she realised his intention, and gripped his hair, but his tongue was already probing between her silken folds the sensations he was arousing so utterly incredible that her cry of denial faltered.

'Relax, and I will show you what you've clearly been denied by your previous lovers,' he promised thickly.

Mortified, she tried to bring her legs together. But he held them apart and dipped his head once more, the skilled flick of his tongue making her whimper with pleasure. 'You can't,' she pleaded. But he could, and did, and when his lips closed around the tiny, ultra-sensitive nub of her clitoris she sobbed his name and dug her nails into his shoulders, clinging to him as ripples of delight began deep inside her.

He moved swiftly to position himself over her, lifted her hips and drove his powerful erection deep into her, thrusting fast and hard and driving her ever upwards. And now she was almost there, at the place she had sensed the first time he had made love to her. He withdrew almost completely, and then sank into her so deeply that their bodies imploded simultaneously. She gave a startled cry as she experienced wave after wave of ecstasy crashing through her, causing her entire body to tremble with the power of a storm, before slowly ebbing away to leave her spent and utterly replete in his arms.

Dear heaven, she had never known it would be so…so awesome, so astounding. She could not find the words. She curved her hands around Thanos's back, loving the feel of his satiny sweat-slicked skin beneath her palms. He was lying on top of her, his body lax and heavy, but she did not want him to move. The erratic beat of his heart thundering in unison with hers was strangely comforting. Was it possible that in the shattering moments of his climax he had experienced the same feeling that had swamped her—a feeling that their souls had united and soared to a place that was uniquely theirs?

It was just sex, she told herself—awesome, amazing sex. Although admittedly she did not have any other experience to compare it with. But surely it was nothing more than the pairing of two people who were held in the thrall of a powerful sexual chemistry? It would be stupid to allow her emotions to become involved, yet she felt a bond with him that went far beyond the physical intimacy they had shared.

Thanos finally rolled onto his back and stared blindly up at the ceiling, more stunned than he cared to admit by the power of the passion they had just shared, the feeling of oneness that he had never experienced with any other woman. It made no sense. He despised Tahlia, and his contempt for her had intensified when she had agreed to sell herself to him. But instead of telling her what he thought of her he had succumbed to the temptation of her fragile beauty and taken her to bed. Lust had made a fool of him, and now his hatred of himself threatened to choke him. He was no better than his father, he acknowledged bitterly. Kosta Savakis had fallen for the charms of an immoral woman and had abandoned his family for his mistress. And now he, Thanos, had sacrificed his self-respect and had sex with the woman who had broken his sister's heart.

He had bought her, he reminded himself grimly as he swung his legs over the side of the bed, not sparing her a glance as he strode into the *en suite* bathroom. Tahlia was a whore, and he was paying a fortune for her. It would have been damnably disappointing if the sex *hadn't* been good. He stood beneath the shower, but the powerful spray did nothing to ease his tension. Sex with Tahlia hadn't just been good, it had been the best he'd ever had, he conceded. He was already hardening again, anticipation licking through his veins as he snatched a towel and roughly dried his body.

But when he returned to the bedroom he discovered her curled up beneath the sheet, one hand beneath her cheek, her long gold lashes making crescents against her flushed skin. Once again he was struck by her air of innocence, and something indefinable tugged in his gut when he saw a single tear slip silently down her face. The sight of her vulnerability shook him to the core, and in moment of absolute clarity his brain finally accepted what his soul had instinctively known when he had joined his body with hers. He was aware of a curious drumming in his ears, and realised that it was the sound of his blood pounding through his veins. His logical mind grasped at straws, recalling all the tabloid stories he had read about her torrid love-life, but when she lifted her lashes and he saw the hurt in her eyes his heart accepted the truth.

'You were a virgin, weren't you?' he said quietly.

She did not reply, but the sudden flare of colour on her pale cheeks filled him with guilt and remorse, and a whole host of other emotions he could not define.

Anger at his crass stupidity swept through him, and his throat felt as though he had swallowed glass as he rasped, 'Why the hell didn't you tell me?'

CHAPTER SIX

THE look of fury on Thanos's face inflamed Tahlia's temper and she sat up, glaring at him as she dragged the sheet across her breasts and pushed her hair over her shoulders. 'What would have been the point?' she demanded bitterly. 'You thought I was an immoral slut who had seduced your sister's husband as well as half the male population of London. Would you have believed me if I'd admitted that I was completely inexperienced?'

Somehow her defiant tone, and the way she hastily dashed her tears away with the back of her hand, emphasised her innocence—an innocence he had taken with all the finesse of a boor, Thanos thought grimly, regret searing him as he recalled his impatience when he had made love to her.

'Probably not,' he conceded honestly. 'But *Theos mou…*' He raked his hand through his hair, his frustration palpable. 'Melina found you in bed with James Hamilton.'

'I told you I didn't sleep with him.'

But he hadn't believed her. He had assumed, as Melina had, that Tahlia and James were lovers, Thanos acknowledged. And during the long hours he had sat at Melina's hospital bedside his hatred of Tahlia had made him determined to seek revenge for the pain he had thought she had caused his sister.

'How do you explain all the stories written about you in the tabloids?' he demanded. 'For the past few months rarely a day has gone by without a picture in the British newspapers of you and one of your seemingly inexhaustible supply of boyfriends at yet another social event.'

'I only went to the parties to promote Reynolds Gems,' Tahlia defended herself. 'My father persuaded me to front an advertising campaign, and then he thought it would give a personal touch if people saw me wearing the company's products. Those men weren't my boyfriends. They were male models hired from an agency. It was all part of the image,' she explained, when Thanos looked sceptical. 'I was photographed by the press wearing couture gowns that were loaned to me by design houses and fabulous jewellery from the Reynolds Gems collection, escorted by a handsome partner. But there was never any romance. Most of the models were too in love with themselves,' she added with a grimace.

'So your party princess image was just a PR stunt?' Thanos gave a harsh laugh. He had certainly been convinced that Tahlia was a good-time girl, and he was still struggling to accept that he had unwittingly stolen her virginity. 'What about the other married actor, Damian Casson? Do you expect me to believe that the photos of the two of you leaving a hotel together were also to promote Reynolds Gems?'

'I don't give a damn what you believe,' Tahlia snapped. 'Damian set me up to make his wife jealous, and as I already told you my solicitor has threatened the papers involved with legal action unless they retract their story of our supposed affair. I hate being in the public eye,' she admitted. 'But I would have done anything to help my father. I just wish all those hours I spent on the PR campaign had done some good.'

'It would have taken a miracle to turn around Reynolds' fortunes,' Thanos told her bluntly. 'Your father had made a catalogue of terrible decisions in recent years, and with the current economic crisis bankruptcy was almost inevitable.

'It wasn't his fault.' Tahlia sprang to her father's defence. 'My mother has been seriously ill, and Dad was so busy caring for her that he couldn't concentrate on running the company. He was terrified he was going to lose her…we both were,' she said huskily, emotion clogging her throat as she acknowledged how afraid she had been that her mother would die.

That fear had haunted her every day of the past two years, and it was only now her mother was well again that she realised how much of a strain it had been to keep smiling and encouraging her parents to think positively when inside she had been racked with worry. Tears stung her eyes and she blinked furiously to dispel them. She had cried on the day her mother had been diagnosed, but since then she had suppressed her emotions and focused on helping her mother through her treatment. Now it felt as though a dam inside her had burst, and two years' worth of tears were flooding out.

She desperately did not want to cry in front of Thanos, and she stared down at the sheets while she tried to regain her composure. But the weeks and months of worry about her mother's health, and her fears that her father could lose his company, combined with the emotional trauma of giving her virginity to a man who despised her, had shattered her tenuous hold on her self-control, and she buried her face in her hands in a frantic attempt to muffle the sound of her weeping.

Once the storm had begun, it raged out of control. She did not know how long she cried, and was only vaguely aware of the mattress dipping as Thanos dropped down onto the bed beside her. She stiffened when she felt his hand on her shoulder, unbearably embarrassed by her breakdown but unable to check the sobs that still tore through her body. Her chest hurt, and her head felt as though it were about to explode, but the hand on her shoulder slid up her neck to massage her nape in a soothing motion that gradually calmed her.

'I'm sorry,' she choked at last, scrubbing her eyes with the back of her hand and staring fixedly into her lap, so mortified by her outburst that she could not bring herself to meet his gaze. 'I'm not usually so pathetic.'

The hand on her neck continued its gentle stroking, and when she dared to glance up she discovered that Thanos had donned a black bathrobe and was sitting so close to her that she could see the tiny lines that fanned around his eyes. He was watching her impassively, but she was startled to glimpse the faintest hint of compassion in their depths.

'What was wrong with your mother?' he asked quietly

'She had breast cancer. It was a particularly aggressive form of the disease, and her initial prognosis was not good.' Tahlia took a shaky breath, shocked by the ferocity of the storm that had ripped through her. 'She had surgery immediately to remove the tumour, followed by intensive chemotherapy which left her desperately weak.' She swallowed, wondering why she was confiding in Thanos, but the words kept tumbling out.

'At one point it seemed that she would not survive the treatment, but somehow she found the strength to keep fighting. My father did everything he could to help her; he went to every chemo session with her, and we took it in turns to sleep in a chair by her bed every time she went into hospital. It's strange how those few hours before dawn seem to last for ever,' she said in a low tone. 'You can't sleep, but you dare not move away from the bed, and as the first light glimmers between the blinds you pray that this is the day there will be some improvement, a turning point.'

'Yes.' Thanos's voice was harsh, and she jerked her head up, catching her breath at the agony etched on his face. 'And every evening, when all hope has gone from that day, you pray that tomorrow will bring the sign you have been waiting for. And so it goes on, day after day. In Melina's case, week after week.'

Tahlia's hand flew to her mouth. How could she have been so crass as to bring up the subject of hospitals when Thanos's sister had been in a coma for weeks? She tensed, expecting him to be angry with her again, and accepted that in all honesty she could not blame him. Since she had learned about the accident she had been tormented by guilt that she should have run after Melina—although it was difficult to imagine what she could have said to the young Greek woman. Even if she had managed to convince Melina she had not known James was married, nothing would have changed the fact that he was a liar and a cheat.

'I can only imagine how awful it must have been,' she said softly, her heart clenching as she pictured Thanos's vigil at his sister's bedside. 'Did other members of your family come to the hospital to wait with you?'

He shrugged. 'I have no other family. My parents died when Melina was five years old, leaving me to bring her up. At first my aunt helped to look after her, but she was elderly and passed away a few months later. Then it was just the two of us.' A nerve flickered in his cheek and he looked away from Tahlia, battling to bring his emotions under control. 'There were times when Melina showed no sign of coming out of her coma and I feared I would be the only surviving member of the Savakis family.'

He must have felt so alone, Tahlia thought gently. As powerless as she had felt as she had watched her mother struggle with the illness that could so easily have ended her life. Instinctively she placed her hand over his, but when he stiffened she realised how stupid her action had been. Thanos now had irrefutable proof that she had not been his brother-in-law's mistress, but she was sure he still blamed her for Melina's accident. She expected him to reject her sympathy, and she made to snatch her hand back. But to her shock he curled his tanned fingers around her paler ones and held her prisoner.

'How is your mother now?'

'Completely recovered—thankfully. Actually, her recovery is a miracle—even her consultant says so,' Tahlia said with a ghost of a smile. 'Dad was overjoyed when we heard the news.' She swallowed the lump in her throat as she recalled how her father had wept tears of relief when he had phoned her with the news. 'That's why it seemed so...so *cruel* that on the same day Mum was given the all-clear Dad learned that Carlton House was in danger of being repossessed by the bank. He took out a mortgage on the house to finance Reynolds Gems,' she explained when Thanos frowned. 'My mother has no idea of the situation. She thinks they are going to enjoy a wonderful retirement in the house that has been in her family for generations. And that's exactly what's going to happen,' she added fiercely. 'My parents have been through two years of hell, and now they deserve to be happy. Dad was so relieved when he heard that Vantage Investments were prepared to buy Reynolds because it meant that he could pay back the bank loan and the mortgage, and Carlton would be safe...'

'And that is why—after you learned that Vantage is a subsidiary of Savakis Holdings, and I made it clear that I had no intention of saving Reynolds Gems—you agreed to sell yourself to me?' Thanos suggested grimly.

Tahlia bit her lip, sensing his renewed anger. 'Yes.'

'*Theos!*' he exploded, aware of a curious hollow sensation in his stomach. 'Why didn't you tell me your parents were in danger of losing their home?

Tahlia gave him a puzzled look. 'Why would you have cared? You made it clear that you would never help my father.

Time was running out, and I knew I would never find another buyer for Reynolds before the bank seized Carlton. The only thing I had to trade was my body,' she finished huskily.

The silence that fell between them simmered with tension. Thanos could not bring himself to look at Tahlia as guilt at the way he had misjudged her surged through him. Far from being an immoral slut, like his father's mistress, it seemed that she was a devoted daughter who had been desperate to help her parents. Her motivation in agreeing to be his mistress had not been to ensure her own financial security but to prevent her parents from being evicted from their home. And she had made the ultimate sacrifice, he thought bleakly. She had given him her virginity, aware that his motivation for taking her to bed was to seek revenge for a crime she had not committed.

He closed his eyes, shutting out the image of her pale, tear-stained face. In the name of heaven, what had he done?

'How did you meet James Hamilton?' he asked abruptly.

Tahlia shot him a startled glance. 'A friend of mine was starring in a play, and James was a member of the cast. We got chatting when I went backstage after the performance, and he…swept me off my feet.' She shook her head, remembering the buzz she had felt when James had singled her out. 'He was handsome, charming, funny… My mother was desperately ill, and I was sick with worry about her, but when I was with James he made me forget my fears for a few hours. I hadn't dated anyone in the years since Michael died,' she explained quietly. 'I was devastated by his death. He was so young and vibrant. We weren't lovers, but our friendship had been developing into something deeper, and I was heartbroken to lose him. For a long time after he died I blamed myself. I had thought he was suffering from the flu virus that was going around the university campus, and by the time I realised that it was something much more serious it was too late. Michael died a few hours after being admitted to hospital.' Her eyes darkened with pain as she remembered the horror of that day.

'When I met James, he was so energetic and full of life—just as Michael had been—and I felt that nothing bad could happen while I was with him.' She bit her lip. 'It never crossed my mind that he could be married. He even took me back to his flat a few times, and it was a typical bachelor pad—there was no sign that Melina lived there.'

'She didn't,' Thanos said heavily. 'I bought her and James an apartment in Athens for a wedding present, and she remained in Greece while he went to England for two months to star in that play. When his contract was extended Melina flew to London to join him. She was immediately suspicious that he was being unfaithful, but instead of confiding in me she read the text messages he'd sent you on his mobile phone, discovered that James had arranged to spend the weekend with you at a hotel, and decided to confront you.'

In her mind Tahlia saw Thanos's sister, standing in the doorway of the hotel suite, the look of shock on her face mirrored in James Hamilton's eyes. But where Melina's expression had been one of utter devastation, James had simply looked annoyed that he had been caught out.

'Poor Melina,' she whispered. 'She must have been distraught. I understand why you blamed me. I *would* have become James's lover that night,' she told Thanos, forcing herself to meet his gaze. 'He'd told me that he loved me, and I thought I loved him. Mum's illness had cast a shadow over everything, and James was the one person who could make me smile. I needed him, and I overlooked things like the fact that he always wanted to borrow money from me.' She swallowed. 'I was a fool, and because of my naïveté Melina almost lost her life. No wonder you hate me,' she said thickly. 'I will always feel guilty that I didn't go after her.'

No one could fake the level of emotion evident in Tahlia's voice, Thanos brooded. The pain she felt at James's treachery was as genuine as her sympathy for Melina. Shame burned like acid in his gut at the way he had treated her. He should not have brought her to Mykonos and forced her to share his bed, and now that he knew what a terrible mistake he had made he should send her back to England immediately. But hard on the heels of that thought came the unsettling realisation that he did not want to let her go.

Guilt filled him with a sudden restlessness, and he stood up and strode over to the window, staring out at the black sky and the silver moonlight dancing on the sea.

'You have nothing to feel guilty about,' he said gruffly. 'James duped you and Melina, and clearly he broke your heart as well as hers.'

Tahlia's heartbeat quickened. 'You believe me?' she asked shakily, shocked by how much his answer mattered.

He swung round from the window, the glow from the bedside lamp casting shadows over his hard-boned face, making his expression unfathomable.

'Yes, I believe you,' he said heavily. 'I'm sorry I misjudged you so badly. But when I first saw Melina in the hospital and learned the extent of her injuries I wanted to kill the two people I believed were responsible for her accident. Now I know you were not to blame, and I bitterly regret forcing you into this damnable deal.'

He walked back over to the bed, his mouth twisting when he saw Tahlia stiffen. *Theos*, he must have terrified her, he thought bleakly, remorse tearing at his insides when he recalled the demands he had made on her untutored body. Her hesitancy should have warned him of her innocence, but she had responded to him with such intense passion that he had believed she was as sexually experienced as the newspaper stories about her had suggested.

As Thanos came closer Tahlia was startled by the almost haggard expression in his eyes, and she felt a pang of compassion for him. How awful it must have been for him to come so close to losing his sister, who was his only living relative. He had cared for Melina since she was a small child, and she could understand how angry he must have felt that she had been hurt. It was understandable that his anger had turned into a quest for revenge.

'You didn't force me into anything,' she said softly. 'You simply offered me the opportunity to ensure my parents can keep their home and I took it. I knew what I was getting into.'

Thanos gave her a level look. 'Patently you did not,' he murmured, and a feeling he could not define stirred deep inside him when her cheeks flooded with colour. 'I deeply regret that I did not know I was your first lover. My impatience to take you to bed made me brutal, and I probably scared the life out of you.' He paused, and then said in a low tone, 'But, in all honesty, I cannot say I am sorry for making love to you. The sexual alchemy between us was obvious from the moment we met at the art gallery, and despite knowing who you were, the role I thought you had played in my sister's accident, I desired you more than I have ever wanted any woman.

'I still do,' he said harshly. 'The deal we made still stands. I am prepared to buy out Reynolds Gems and save your father from financial ruin in return for your agreement to remain here on Mykonos as my mistress until the end of the month.'

He wanted her to stay with him. Tahlia was shocked by the heady relief that swept through her, but it was quickly followed by a hollow feeling of despair. Making love with Thanos had been an incredible experience that she would never forget; not simply because it had been her first time, but because the feel of his satiny skin beneath her fingertips and the exquisite brush of his mouth caressing every inch of her body were imprinted on her brain for all time. One night was all it had taken for her to be utterly captivated by him. What would she be like after a month as his mistress—when he dismissed her from his life?

Surely it would be better for her to leave him now? To walk away with her pride restored and forget the deal that had turned her into the wanton creature she had become in his arms? But her father's financial problems still remained, and until the buy-out of Reynolds Gems was completed Carlton House was still at risk of repossession. Nothing had changed—except that Thanos was no longer looking at her with contempt in his eyes.

He sat back down on the bed and trailed his finger lightly over her cheek, the sudden warmth in his eyes making Tahlia's heart lurch. 'The passion we shared tonight was beyond anything I have ever known with any other woman. I was blinded by my anger, and determined to take revenge for the heartbreak I believed you had caused Melina, but I was wrong about you. Can we start over?' he asked quietly. 'Whatever this is between us, it is nowhere close to burning out—not for either of us, is it?'

She wanted to deny it—wished she could coolly thank him for initiating her into the pleasures of sex before she caught the first flight home. But the words would not come, and her breath snagged in her throat as he slowly lowered his head until his mouth was a whisper away from hers.

'Stay with me, Tahlia? Please?'

She must have taken leave of her senses, but she could not resist him. That had been her trouble right from the start, she acknowledged as she sagged against him and parted her lips beneath the gentle pressure of his. The slow, sweet kiss was like nothing she had ever experienced before, and the element of gentleness tugged at her heart. When he curved his arms around her she slid her hands up to his nape, and the familiar melting warmth started low in her pelvis as he deepened the kiss to another level and desire swiftly built to a crescendo of need.

She was sure he would ease her down onto the pillows, and she slid her fingers into his hair to guide him down on top of her. But to her disbelief he lifted his head, his eyes darkening a fraction as he saw the confusion in hers.

'Wait here.' He dropped a light kiss on her still parted lips and strode into the *en suite* bathroom.

Had he been playing with her? she wondered sickly, clutching the sheet to her. Did he want to demonstrate that *he* would call the shots in any relationship they might have? She must have been out of her mind to have agreed to stay with him, she thought wildly.

But while she was debating whether to get up and pack her suitcase before she informed him that she wanted to leave after all, he re-entered the bedroom.

'What are you doing?' she gasped when he flicked the sheet out of her grasp and leaned over to scoop her into his arms.

'I've run you a bath. I have a feeling you ache in places you didn't know existed,' he murmured, chuckling when she blushed scarlet.

'I can take care of myself,' she muttered, when he shouldered open the door to the bathroom and carried her over to the huge marble bath filled to the brim with fragrant bubbles.

'Humour me, hmm…?' There was a hint of steel beneath his soft tone, and before she had time to argue the point he lowered her into the water.

It felt blissful, Tahlia acknowledged as she leaned her head back against the padded neck support and closed her eyes.

Thanos had been right; she had discovered muscles that were previously unused. But the memory of how he had driven into her over and over again until she had reached the pinnacle of pleasure caused molten heat to unfurl deep in her pelvis. Shocked by the erotic imagery, she let her eyes fly open to discover that he had shrugged out of his robe and was standing naked and unashamedly aroused by the side of the bath. The flickering light from the dozens of candles around the room gave his body a satin sheen, and her gaze moved down, following the path of crisp dark hairs that covered his chest and arrowed over his flat stomach. He was a work of art, she thought shakily, as she dropped her eyes lower still and absorbed the awesome power of his masculinity.

'Look at me like that for much longer and I won't be responsible for my actions,' he warned softly, his slow smile stealing her breath.

How could she ever have thought that his eyes were cold? she wondered, her heartbeat quickening when he stepped into the bath and sat opposite her, drawing her towards him so that she was aware of the muscular strength of his thighs holding her prisoner. Not that she wanted to escape, she acknowledged ruefully, giving a little gasp when he skimmed his hands over her ribs and cupped her breasts in his hands, the delicate brush of his thumb pads across her nipples sending exquisite shafts of sensation spiralling through her.

'How can I wash when you're doing that?' she mumbled, her eyes locked on the sensual curve of his mouth as he slowly lowered his head and claimed her lips in a long, drugging kiss that stoked the fire inside her to an inferno.

'Allow me to help you.' He picked up a bar of soap and smoothed it over her shoulders, breasts, stomach and thighs, with such dedication to detail that she made a muffled sound in her throat.

'I'm sure I'm clean. You can stop now,' she said huskily, her eyes widening in shock when he discarded the soap and slipped his hand between her legs, parting her with gentle skill and sliding a finger deep inside her. Moist heat flooded through her as he stretched her wider and slipped another digit into her, his fingers moving in an erotic dance that drove her higher and higher towards an orgasm.

'Do you want me to stop, *agape*?' he queried gently as he brushed his thumb pad delicately over the tight nub of her clitoris. Sensation speared her and she arched her hips, nothing in her mind now but desperation for him to give her the release she craved.

'No. Don't stop…please…' She groaned when he withdrew his fingers, and clutched his shoulders when he stood and swung her into his arms before climbing out of the bath. Water streamed from their bodies and dripped onto the carpet as he strode into the bedroom, but he seemed unconcerned that her wet hair soaked through the bedspread as he placed her on the bed and stretched out next to her, his mouth capturing hers in a kiss of pure possession.

'This time we'll take it slowly,' he promised, pausing to swiftly don protection before he nudged her legs apart and moved over her.

Tahlia appreciated the care and consideration he showed as he eased the solid length of his erection into her, but as he filled her, inch by tantalising inch, she discovered that she did not want him to be gentle. Her desire for him was as fierce as a forest fire blazing out of control, and she wanted him to make love to her with the same savage passion that had overwhelmed them both the first time he had possessed her.

She was too shy to voice her need for him, but instead she moved with him, arching her hips to meet each powerful thrust and digging her fingers into his shoulders to urge him to take her faster, harder...

'*Theos*, Tahlia, I don't want to hurt you,' he growled, fighting to retain his self-control.

'You won't. I want you.' Words could not express the depths of her passion, the throbbing ache of her need for him to take her to the heights, but when his lips claimed hers she kissed him hungrily, sliding her tongue into his mouth so that he groaned and tensed before increasing the power of each thrust into her eager body.

Thalia clung to his damp shoulders and tossed her head from side to side, feeling the first spasms building inside her growing, growing until they were an unstoppable force, and she gave a thin, animal cry as her body arched with the explosive force of her climax.

Thanos felt the delicious tightening of her muscles around his shaft and gritted his teeth, determined that this time he would remain in control. He slid his hands beneath her buttocks and tilted her hips, driving into her with deep, steady strokes, taking her higher again, until she sobbed his name and raked her fingers on the silk bedspread. Only when she had climaxed for the third time did his restraint slip, and he paused, savouring the anticipation of the pleasure to come, before he gave one last powerful thrust and experienced the shattering ecstasy of release.

Long moments passed before his breathing returned to normal. He rolled off her and immediately drew her into his arms, frowning when he caught the glimmer of tears on her lashes. 'Forgive me,' he said deeply. 'I was afraid I would hurt you. It was too much, too soon. I should have curbed my impatience.'

Tahlia shook her head, blinking back the tears she had hoped he would not see and giving him a brilliant smile that evoked a peculiar feeling in his chest. 'I was impatient too,' she assured him, and then to her surprise could not prevent herself from yawning so widely that Thanos chuckled, the sound echoing beneath her ear as he curved his arm around her and settled her against him.

'And now you are tired. Go to sleep, *agape*,' he bade her softly, when she opened her mouth to deny it. Her lashes were already drifting down, and Thanos was shaken by the unexpected surge of protectiveness that swept through him as he watched her fall asleep.

CHAPTER SEVEN

Tahlia was awoken by the bright sunlight filtering through the blinds. She turned her head and found that she was alone, the faint indentation on the pillow beside her the only indication that Thanos had slept in the bed last night. That and the slight tenderness of her breasts, the ache of muscles never previously used…

She blushed as she recalled in vivid detail the passion they had shared. Sex with Thanos had been a revelation, and in all honesty she did not regret that he was her first lover. The incredible sensuality of their lovemaking was proof that it was possible to enjoy physical intimacy without emotional involvement—because of course her emotions were *not* involved, she assured herself. Sexual chemistry was a powerful force and she had been unable to resist its pull. Yet she was conscious of a dull ache around her heart that had nothing to do with the pleasurable excesses of the previous night.

The most important thing was that Carlton House was safe and her parents would be able to spend their retirement free from financial worries, she told herself firmly as she threw back the sheets and headed for the *en suite* bathroom. It was ridiculous to wonder what would have happened if she and Thanos had simply been two strangers who had met one evening and been instantly attracted to one another. Perhaps he would have invited her out to dinner or the theatre? Would they have gone the conventional route of dating for a while before their relationship progressed to the bedroom?

It would not have been long before their mutual sexual awareness had exploded into passion, she thought with a rueful smile. But she wished they'd had the chance to get to know one another, to become friends before they became lovers. Instead their relationship was a business arrangement, and although Thanos no longer seemed to despise her, there was no escaping the fact that he was paying for her to share his bed.

The sun was already hot when she stepped onto the terrace, and she was glad of the shade cast by the large parasol as she sat down to breakfast. A note propped up against the coffee pot informed her that Thanos would be in meetings until late afternoon, and, recalling his scathing comments about her lack of clothes, she decided to go shopping in Mykonos Town.

'Yes, there is a bus,' the maid told her, looking puzzled when Tahlia asked her for directions to the town. 'But Mr Savakis would not expect you to take a bus. His chauffeur will drive you wherever you want to go.'

'The bus will be fine,' Tahlia replied cheerfully. She could not rationalise why she did not want to make use of Thanos's personal staff. It was simply important that she retained her independence as much as possible.

Using public transport also meant that she had an excellent tour of the island, she discovered an hour later, as the bus sped along the road. She stared at the rocky hilltops where goats were grazing, and then turned her head to admire the stunning view of the sea. On the horizon she could see the famous windmills, standing like sentinels on the hills above the port, and as the bus wound down into the town centre she was entranced by the myriad square white, flat-roofed houses, jumbled together in impossibly narrow streets.

Even this early in the season the town was bustling with tourists who strolled along the rows of souvenir shops and sat beneath brightly coloured parasols outside the cafés and tavernas. Mykonos was one of the most cosmopolitan of the Greek Islands, and unfortunately this was reflected in the price tags inside the fashionable boutiques. Determined not to allow Thanos to buy her clothes, Tahlia spent the last of her savings, earmarked to pay her electricity bill, on two evening dresses which she did not particularly like but were the cheapest she could find.

She spent another enjoyable hour window-shopping, had lunch in a charming little restaurant in an area of the town called Little Venice, where the buildings were so close to the sea that the balconies overhung the water, and finally caught the bus back to the Artemis, feeling hot and weary, but satisfied that she had two suitable outfits to replace the blouse that Thanos had ruined.

She was surprised to see him standing by the French doors when she walked into the suite, and his grim expression as he swung round to face her made Tahlia's heart sink.

'Where have you been for the past five hours?' he queried tersely. 'The maid said you went out at eleven this morning,' he added, when Tahlia frowned and checked her watch.

'I can't believe I was out for so long. I went into the town, and there was so much to see. Time just flew,' she said defensively.

'Particularly as you travelled by bus,' Thanos said disapprovingly. 'The maid told me she had explained to you that I have assigned a driver to act as your personal chauffeur. Yianis would have given you a tour of the island—and carried your shopping,' he added, his eyes dropping to the bags she was holding. 'I was beginning to worry that something had happened to you,' he said tensely. 'You are a stranger to Mykonos, and some of the bars are not good places for you to go on your own.'

Tahlia's temper prickled at the note of censure in his voice. 'I'm a big girl now, and I can take care of myself.'

Did she have any idea how young she looked, with her face bare of make-up and her hair caught up in a ponytail? Thanos mused. He could imagine the interest she had aroused among the male population of Mykonos in her faded denim shorts and a white strap top, beneath which she was clearly not wearing a bra, and he felt a caveman instinct to lock her away in the highest tower.

'During my student days I spent two summers backpacking around Europe. I know the kind of seedy places to avoid. I worked in many of them,' she admitted ruefully.

'Doing what?' Thanos asked curiously.

'Waitressing, mainly—although I did try a brief stint cooking pancakes in a crêperie in Spain. Until I set light to the kitchen and the manager sacked me,' Tahlia told him cheerfully. 'I was better at bar-work, or cleaning. Often I worked seventy hours a week, and saved the money I earned to see me through my next term at university.'

Thanos frowned. 'Didn't your parents support you financially while you were studying?'

'They couldn't afford to. Carlton House suffered serious structural damage in a storm a few years ago, and the cost of the repairs was astronomical. But I was happy to pay my own way. I never expected hand-outs.'

The Tahlia he was getting to know was nothing like the image fostered in the tabloids of a spoilt party-girl, Thanos brooded, trying to picture her waiting on tables. He remembered the exhaustion of working ridiculously long hours as a labourer, struggling to earn enough to pay the bills and feed and clothe Melina. Memories of those years of poverty were the reason why he now made regular donations to charities supporting the under-privileged, and they had made him appreciate all that he had. Until now he had never met any woman, apart from his sister, who respected the value of money.

'But presumably your parents paid for your flat? You could not have afforded to buy a property in such an affluent area of London on the money you earned as a waitress.'

'Oh, the flat isn't mine, it belongs to George. My aunt Georgina,' Tahlia explained hastily, when Thanos's brows drew together. 'I moved in with her after I left university. She's elderly, and had had several falls. I wanted to take care of her, but sadly she developed dementia and it got to the point where I was terrified of leaving her to go to work because she had so many accidents. After she left a plastic jug on the electric hotplate and the kitchen caught fire my parents and I decided that it would be better for her to move into a residential home where she could have full-time care. I visit her twice a week—' Tahlia broke off at the realisation that she would be unable to visit her aunt for the next month. 'I don't suppose she'll miss me,' she said quietly. 'She doesn't recognise me any more.'

'Yet you still visit her regularly?' Thanos murmured.

'Of course.' Tahlia shrugged. 'Dementia is a cruel illness, but it doesn't define Aunt George. She's still a wonderful person.'

Far from being heartless, as he had once believed, Tahlia clearly possessed a depth of compassion and kindness that he had never found in any other woman, Thanos acknowledged. He did not want to dwell on how he had misjudged her and he strolled towards her, glancing curiously at her shopping bags.

'So, what did you buy?'

'Clothes—as ordered,' she replied brightly. 'Two evening dresses, to be precise.' She pulled a garish pink gown from one of the bags and held it up for his inspection. 'What do you think?'

'I think you had better show me the other one,' he said flatly.

'If you don't like the pink, I thought I couldn't go wrong with classic black.' Tahlia held the plain black dress against her and gave an impatient sigh when he shook his head. 'What's wrong with it?'

'It's cheap, badly made, and it drains the colour from your face,' Thanos told her bluntly. He lifted his hand and ran his finger lightly down her cheek, watching the soft flush of rose-pink stain her skin. 'If they are the only two choices, then I have to say that I definitely prefer you wearing no clothes at all, *agape*.'

The sultry gleam in his eyes caused a delicious little shiver to run through Tahlia, and her breath snagged in her throat when he slid the strap of her cotton top over her shoulder. It would be so easy to close the few inches between them and tilt her head in readiness for his kiss, but she was suddenly gripped with shyness. She was here with him to fulfil her side of a business arrangement, she reminded herself fiercely. She had not expected to be so utterly captivated by him—or to feel this lingering regret that their relationship would never be more than sex.

'I think I'll hit the shower,' she mumbled. 'It was hot and dusty in town.'

She quickly made her escape, crossing the lounge to the bedroom and carrying on into the *en suite* bathroom. A long, tepid shower cooled her heated skin and went some way to restoring her equilibrium. When she'd finished she wound a towel sarong-like around her body and blasted her hair with the hairdrier, wondering if Thanos had returned to work.

The sight of him propped up in bed halted her in her tracks, and her heart missed a beat as her eyes travelled down from his bare muscular chest, covered with whorls of dark hair, to the sheet draped low over his hips. The word handsome did not do justice to his stunning looks and simmering virility. One look at him was all it took for her to melt, she thought despairingly, unable to tear her eyes from the sensual promise of his mouth. The feral heat in his gaze was both an invitation and a demand, and when he wordlessly flicked back the sheet to reveal the awesome strength of his arousal, she swallowed, her eyes locked with his as she walked slowly towards the bed.

Heart pounding so hard she was sure he must hear it, she stretched out beside him, her faint sigh muffled as he lowered his head and claimed her mouth in a slow, drugging kiss that sparked a flame inside her. His tongue probed between her lips, demanding access as he deepened the kiss, and she responded mindlessly, her body quivering with delight. He unwrapped her towel and stroked his hand over her breasts, teasing her nipples into hard peaks before he replaced his fingers with his mouth and laved each dusky tip until she gasped with pleasure.

Passion built swiftly, and when he slipped his hand between her thighs she spread her legs wider, heard his low groan of approval as he parted her and discovered the slick wetness of her arousal.

'You can touch me too,' Thanos murmured, smiling when colour stained her cheeks.

After a moment's hesitation she complied, and tested his restraint to its limit when she stroked her fingers lightly along his swollen length and then grew bolder and encircled him. Her innocence was indisputable, but she was an apt pupil, he acknowledged, his heart racing as he reached for a protective sheath and then positioned himself over her. He entered her with slow deliberation, watching her eyes widen as she felt him slide deeper, filling her to the hilt before he withdrew almost fully and thrust again, establishing a rhythm that drove them both to the edge and over, as their passion exploded in the glory of mutual climax.

It was just good sex, he reminded himself when he finally withdrew and rolled onto his back, taking her with him and tangling his hand in her hair. He guided her mouth down on his and kissed her with lazy appreciation. Physical compatibility at its best—which left him with a feeling of contentment that he had never experienced with any other woman.

'I need to work for another couple of hours,' he told her as he pulled on his trousers. 'This evening we're attending a reception. The shipping magnate Christos Petrelis is hosting a party on his private island.'

'Which dress shall I wear?' Tahlia mused. 'The black or the pink?'

He gave her a level look. 'Neither.'

'You think I should go nude?' she teased him, her impish smile tugging faintly on his heart.

'It would certainly be an attention-stealer, but I admit I like the fact that I am the only man who has ever seen your naked body,' he told her, frowning slightly as he acknowledged a degree of possessiveness that was unexpected. He reached for his phone and spoke rapidly in Greek before cutting the call. 'Fortunately, I am a much better shopper than you. Come and see.'

Puzzled, Tahlia pulled on her robe and followed him into the lounge. He strode over to the door and opened it, to admit three porters laded with bags and boxes emblazoned with the names of famous design houses.

'What…?' She lifted her eyes to his face and waited for his explanation.

'You need new clothes,' Thanos murmured coolly. 'So I phoned a friend in Paris who is a personal stylist, gave her your measurements and a description of your colouring, and asked her to send over a selection of suitable outfits.'

'Well, you can just send them straight back.' Tahlia stared around at the dozens of boxes and bags, from Chanel, Gucci, Prada, and felt sick with misery. The laughter she had shared with Thanos a few moments earlier had been replaced with a tangible tension. 'I won't wear clothes paid for by you. I told you—I pay my own way and I won't accept hand-outs. Even though they are haute couture,' she added grimly.

Thanos's smile had faded and his expression was unreadable, although Tahlia sensed that she had angered him. 'You will wear them,' he told her, with a note of implacability in his voice that warned her she would have a fight on her hands if she refused. 'As we discussed before, your sole purpose for the next month is to please me, and I expect you to dress appropriately.'

'I don't need reminding that you are paying for me to act the role of your mistress,' she said stiffly, hurt pride churning in her stomach. In a battle of wills he would be a clear winner, and a dignified retreat was her only option. 'Very well, I'll wear the clothes while I am here on Mykonos. But I shall regard them as a uniform, and I will leave them behind when our contract is over.'

Thanos restrained himself from pulling her into his arms and shaking some sense into her, and ignored the stronger urge to kiss her into submission. 'Suit yourself,' he said laconically, snatching up his jacket from the back of the chair and heading for the door. 'I believe Monique included a Valentino evening gown in the collection. Wear that tonight,' he ordered, and he stepped into the corridor and slammed the door behind him without giving her the chance to argue further.

Tahlia worked off her fury at Thanos's high-handedness by swimming thirty lengths in the private pool. When she returned to the bedroom she discovered that the maid had un-packed the clothes and hung them in the wardrobe: beautiful classical evening dresses, elegant trousers, skirts and tops, all with matching shoes and accessories, and a variety of exqui-site nightgowns and sets of lacy underwear which were nothing like the plain cotton bras and knickers she usually wore.

Presumably Thanos believed that as he was paying for her he could indulge in a typical male fantasy of seeing her in flimsy scraps of silk and lace, she thought dully as she held up a low-cut black basque complete with silk ribbons which laced up at the front. In different circumstances she would have taken huge delight in a cupboard full of designer outfits, but the knowledge that Thanos had bought them emphasised the fact that she was—as he had pointed out—here to please him.

The Valentino dress *was* stunning, she was forced to admit later, after she had taken a leisurely bath and smoothed fragrant body lotion onto her skin before dressing for the party. The heather-coloured silk gown left her shoulders bare and clung lovingly to her waist and hips, the side-split in the skirt reaching to mid-thigh. It was the most daring dress she had ever worn, and as she stared at her reflection in the mirror she barely recognised the sultry seductress looking back at her as sensible Tahlia Reynolds.

Thanos walked into the bedroom as she was spraying perfume to her pulse points. She guessed he must have used the spare bedroom as a dressing room, because he had changed into a black dinner suit which emphasised his lean length and the formidable width of his shoulders. She hated the way her heart jerked as her gaze skittered over the chi-selled beauty of his face.

Her heart thudded as his eyes swept over her.

'You look beautiful.' His voice was as deep and sensuous as crushed velvet, and her senses flared as she caught the drift of his cologne when he strolled over to her. 'I bought this for you to wear tonight.'

Tahlia caught her breath when he held up a large peardrop-shaped amethyst, surrounded by diamonds and suspended on a fine white-gold chain. Before she had time to argue Thanos fastened the pendant around her neck and stood back to admire the sight of the violet-coloured gem sitting in the V between her creamy breasts.

'Perfect,' he murmured, his eyes gleaming with feral hunger as he traced his finger over the pendant and then slipped it lower and settled it between her breasts. 'It matches the colour of your dress exactly. But whenever I look at you this evening I will be imagining you wearing nothing but the necklace,' he added thickly.

The pendant felt heavy on Tahlia's skin, and she was tempted to tear it off. She felt as though he had branded her—as if every time he looked at her he would be reminded that he had paid for her.

'You think you can buy everything, don't you?' she snapped. 'You have so little understanding of the value of money that the cost of a valuable piece of jewellery is irrelevant to you. I suppose that's what comes of being born into wealth,' she finished scathingly.

Thanos's face had darkened at her outburst, and now he gave a mirthless laugh. 'I wasn't born into wealth,' he said harshly. 'There was no grand mansion house in *my* family to pass down through generations. I didn't enjoy a privileged childhood or have the advantage of a private education. I was born on a small island called Agistri, and I grew up in a tiny stone-built house with no running water,' he explained flatly. 'As a youth I assumed that I would spend my life as a goat-herd. I had no expectations of ever moving away from the island where my family had lived for generations.'

'What made you decide to leave?' Tahlia asked, stunned by his revelation that he had not inherited his vast fortune.

'An English woman called Wendy Jones.' Thanos could not disguise the bitterness in his voice. 'She was my father's mistress—and after he walked out on his family and divorced my mother she subsequently became his new wife. Wendy had already been married and divorced twice when she bought a villa on Agistri. She employed my father to carry out renovation work on her house, but it soon became apparent that she wanted him for more than his building skills. A few months after he began working for her he dropped the bombshell to my mother that their marriage was over.

He continued harshly, 'My mother was distraught, especially when my father stopped all financial support. I was fifteen, and Melina was just three years old. I dropped out of school, lied about my age, and managed to pick up some labouring work, using the skills my father had taught me. My mother wept about the disruption to my education, but I had no choice—I couldn't allow her and my sister to starve, and my father was too besotted with his tart to spare a thought for his wife and children. I lost all the respect I had felt for my father,' Thanos said savagely. 'He made a complete fool of himself. Wendy flirted with him outrageously. She knew he was married, but that little fact didn't seem to matter to her. She'd decided that she wanted him for herself and she deliberately pursued him, uncaring that she had ripped my family apart—'

He broke off abruptly, and in the tense silence Tahlia could feel his barely leashed anger. No wonder Thanos had been so ready to believe that she had stolen James Hamilton from his sister, she brooded. His family had been blown apart by his father's mistress. It must have seemed as though history was repeating itself when his sister had discovered that her husband was having an affair.

'I never spoke to my father after he married again,' he continued grimly. 'Eighteen months after the wedding he was killed in a horrific accident. Wendy had insisted on having a swimming pool, and he was crushed when the mechanical digger he was driving overturned.' He ignored Tahlia's shocked gasp and continued. 'My father had not made a will, and everything he owned—namely the house where my mother, Melina and I still lived—passed to his wife. Within a week of his funeral Wendy demanded that we leave her property. It was the final blow to my mother, to be evicted from the home where she had lived for her entire married life by my father's whore. She died of pneumonia six months later, leaving me to care for Melina, who was then just five years old.'

Tahlia tried to imagine Thanos at seventeen—a boy who overnight had had to become a man and take responsibility for his young sister while he was grieving for both his parents. 'You must feel very protective of Melina,' she murmured.

He turned his head and stared at her, his dark eyes blazing. 'I would give my life for her,' he vowed fiercely. 'I promised my mother as she lay dying that I would always take care of Melina. When I first saw her after the accident and I was told she had less than a fifty percent chance of surviving...' His throat moved convulsively. 'I was haunted by the knowledge that I had failed to protect her.'

Tahlia was shocked by the raw emotion in his eyes. There was no doubt that Thanos adored his sister, and she realised that far from being the hard, ruthless man she had once believed his feelings ran deep. If he ever fell in love he would give his heart utterly, she brooded, aware of a faint tug of envy for the woman who might one day win his devotion.

He had fallen silent, seemingly lost in his thoughts, but after a moment he picked up her stole and placed it around her shoulders. 'Are you ready to leave?'

When she nodded, he escorted her out of the suite. To her surprise the lift carried them upwards, and when the doors opened she stepped out onto the roof of the hotel where a helicopter was waiting.

'The chopper is the quickest way to travel between the islands,' he explained as he assisted her into the cockpit. 'I've held a private pilot's licence for ten years. You'll be quite safe.'

Tahlia had always been nervous in the air, but as they took off she had no qualms about Thanos's ability to fly the chopper. Was there nothing this man could not do? she wondered as she watched him manoeuvre the joystick and the helicopter responded smoothly to his control. She glanced out of the window and watched the streaks of pink and gold which flared from a fiery sun as it slipped below the horizon.

Twenty minutes later they landed on the lawn in front of a huge white-walled villa and were escorted inside by a uniformed member of staff.

There was serious money here, Tahlia mused, glancing around at the stunning array of diamonds and designer gowns worn by the predominantly young and blonde women who were being paraded on the arms of their significantly older male companions. Fortunately she was practised in the art of making small-talk with people she had never met before—or was likely to meet again, and she moved around the room with Thanos, sipping champagne and forcing herself to smile until her jaw ached.

She was aware of the envious glances she received from other women, the thinly veiled speculation in their eyes that she would not remain his mistress for long. Thanos Savakis's relationships were notoriously short-lived, but tonight he only had eyes for her, and he kept his arm around her waist, as if he shared her reluctance for them to be apart for even a moment—although that was surely just wishful thinking, Tahlia told herself firmly.

He dominated her mind: a tall, dark and brooding presence at her side. A man who, in a few hours, would take her to bed and make love to her until he had sated his hunger for her. She would not offer any resistance, she thought wearily as his eyes fused with hers and the flare of heat in their depths sent a jolt of awareness down her spine. He had taken her innocence and awoken her sensuality, and she could not deny the desire that he alone aroused in her.

'Dance with me.' His eyes seemed to scorch her soul, and without waiting for her to reply he drew her onto the dance floor and into his arms.

He swamped her senses, the warmth of his body and the sensual musk of his cologne drifting around her so that she relaxed against him and rested her head on his chest, the ache inside her soothed by the steady beat of his heart. When he lowered his head and claimed her mouth she parted her lips and kissed him back with a fervency that caused him to tighten his hold and pull her closer, so that she could feel the throbbing force of his arousal press impatiently into her pelvis.

At last he lifted his mouth from hers and stared down at her quizzically. 'Ready to go?' he queried softly.

The champagne was flooding through her veins, sweeping away her doubts and inhibitions and leaving her weak and boneless and the slow drumbeat of desire was thudding irresistibly deep inside her.

'Yes.'

His eyes darkened, his mouth twisting in a self-derisive grimace as he slid his hand down to her bottom and pulled her up hard against the swollen shaft straining beneath his trousers. 'You are like a fever in my blood, *agape*,' he muttered thickly. 'I am burning up with wanting you.'

The short flight back to Mykonos seemed interminable. The silence grew ever more intense as the lift carried them down a floor to Thanos's suite. The moment they stepped through the door Thanos swept her into his arms and strode into the master bedroom, the purpose in his eyes causing anticipation to coil low in Tahlia's stomach.

She helped him remove her clothes and then his, her heart thudding as she ran her hands through the mass of wiry black hairs that covered his chest and felt the erratic beat of his life-force beneath her fingertips. The solid length of his arousal pushed insistently against her thigh, and she felt the familiar melting warmth between her legs as her body grew impatient for him. She wanted him so desperately that her limbs trembled, and when she tentatively stroked her fingers along his swollen shaft and heard his swiftly indrawn breath she expected him to lift her onto the bed, to possess her with the same raw passion of their previous encounters.

Instead he stroked his hands through her hair, before trailing his fingertips in a butterfly caress along her collarbone and then down to cup her breasts in his palms. His slow smile told her that he understood her impatience, but his movements were unhurried as his mouth claimed hers in a deep, drugging kiss that seared her soul.

It was just good sex, she reminded herself. It meant nothing to him, and she would be a fool to open her heart to him. But when he sank down onto the bed and lifted her over him, guiding her gently down so that she absorbed the full strength of his erection, she looked into his dark eyes and acknowledged on a wave of sheer panic that her heart was in serious danger.

CHAPTER EIGHT

THE prickling sensation on Tahlia's shoulders warned her that she would be wise to move out of the sun. It was almost four p.m., she noted, her stomach tightening as she glanced at her watch. Soon Thanos would come back to the suite, and she would go inside, to the cool, shaded bedroom, where he would make love to her as he had done every day of the past week since they had arrived on Mykonos.

She moved her sunbed beneath the parasol and picked up her book—the third paperback novel she'd read this week—but she could not concentrate on the story, and after a few moments she set it down again, looking towards the French doors. Her heart-rate accelerated when she discovered that he had stepped onto the terrace and was watching her, his expression hidden behind his sunglasses. He dipped his head in silent greeting before walking back inside, and, like a puppet controlled by invisible strings, she stood up and followed him.

When she reached the master bedroom she found him naked, stretched out on the silk sheets like a sultan waiting for his favourite concubine. That was all she was to him, she reminded herself despairingly. But he had treated her with respect and consideration since he had made her his mistress, and day by day she had fallen deeper under his spell.

It was ridiculous to still feel shy when he had explored every inch of her body with his hands and mouth, but she could not bring herself to strip off her bikini, and stood watching him, her eyes unconsciously wary, until he held out his hand and murmured, 'Come here,' in the deep, velvet-soft voice that sent a quiver of longing down her spine.

In the sensual feast that followed he aroused her to a fever-pitch of desire, peeling her bikini from her breasts and hips and probing the moist heat of her femininity with his tongue before he moved over her and possessed her with fierce, powerful thrusts that drove them both to the ecstasy of simultaneous release. Afterwards she lay limply beside him, knowing that he would soon stroll into the shower, before dressing and returning to another of his interminable meetings. But to her surprise he propped himself up on one elbow and stared down at her.

'So, what did you do today?'

She shrugged, puzzled by his unexpected interest. 'Sat in the sun before it got too hot, swam, read a book—the same as I've done every day,' she added, unable to disguise the faint note of frustration in her voice.'

Thanos's eyes narrowed. 'You could go shopping. There are some excellent designer boutiques in the town, and I've told you to use the money I left for you.'

'And I've told you I don't want your money,' Tahlia said fiercely. 'Besides, you've already provided me with more than enough clothes. I don't need to go shopping.'

'Most women I know do not shop out of necessity,' Thanos murmured dryly.

'Well, clearly I'm different to your other women.'

Tahlia's tart comment filled Thanos with a mixture of amusement and frustration. He had made love to her every night—and most afternoons—he acknowledged wryly, and he knew every secret dip and curve of her body. But her mind remained stubbornly closed to him. He was no nearer to understanding what made Tahlia Reynolds tick than he had been a week ago.

He trailed his hand lazily down her body, feeling a spurt of triumph at the sharp catch of her breath as he pushed her legs apart. 'If you are bored, I will have to spend more time… entertaining you,' he drawled.

'It's not possible to have sex any more times than we do already,' she said ruefully. 'But if I spend many more hours sun-bathing I'll turn into a crisp.' She pushed her hair out of her eyes and continued hurriedly, 'Isn't there any office work I could do? Filing, admin…? I don't care what it is, as long as I have something to do. I'm a working girl,' she told him seriously. 'I'm not used to sitting around all day doing nothing.'

Tahlia was so very different from the woman he had believed her to be when he had blamed her for his sister's accident, Thanos acknowledged. During the tense hours he'd spent waiting for Melina to regain consciousness his image of Tahlia had fused with his memories of his father's English mistress, and his hatred of her had grown as intense as the hatred he felt towards the woman who had destroyed his family. But over the past week he had discovered that Tahlia was nothing like the callous, cold-hearted woman his father had married. True, she possessed an unexpectedly fiery temper beneath her gentle exterior, but she was unfailingly polite towards his staff, instinctively kind, and the most generous lover he had ever known.

He had not expected to like her, he conceded, but to his surprise he had found himself thinking about her when his mind should have been concentrating on profit margins, and for the first time in his life he resented the hours he spent in the office because he would rather have been with her.

He got up from the bed, retrieved his clothes from the floor where he had carelessly discarded them, and paused on his way to the *en suite* bathroom to look back at her. The sunlight filtering through the blinds turned her hair to pure gold, falling in a silken sheet around her shoulders, and her skin was still flushed from the passion they had just shared. He must be mad to be considering working with her when she was such a serious distraction to his thought process, he thought wryly, but his logical brain insisted that she could be extremely useful to him.

'I've a meeting scheduled for the next hour. Come to my office after that and we'll discuss an idea I've had which I'm certain will alleviate your boredom,' he murmured, smiling at her look of surprise and striding on into the bathroom before she could question him.

Thanos was standing by a window which afforded a spectacular view of the sea when Tahlia entered his office. 'Take a seat,' he invited, the warmth of his smile doing strange things to her insides.

She quickly sat down in the chair in front of his desk, her eyes drawn to his hard profile, and her composure wavered as she studied his chiselled features, the slashing line of his cheekbone and his square chin. An hour ago, that sensual mouth had traced every inch of her body and lingered in her most secret places to wreak havoc. The memory caused liquid heat to flood through her veins, and she knew from the sudden flare of heat in his eyes that he had read her mind.

'You said you have an idea?' she said hastily, aware that she was blushing.

'I have several,' Thanos assured her throatily, conscious of the familiar tug of desire in his groin as he studied her. She had changed into an elegant cream linen skirt and a white blouse, and looked as chaste as a nun, with her hair drawn back from her face in a neat chignon. But somehow her wholesome, fresh-faced appearance was incredibly sexy. His eyes lingered on her lips, coated in a pale pink gloss, and his heart-rate quickened.

He ruthlessly suppressed the hunger that gnawed in his gut and picked up the folder on his desk. 'However, I think we had better concentrate on the idea I asked you here to discuss. The Artemis is due to open in three weeks' time,' he said abruptly.

Tahlia nodded. 'I'm sure it will be a great success,' she murmured, not sure what the opening date of his new hotel had to do with her.

'I hope so. We're fully booked for the whole of the summer, but it's vital we make an excellent first impression. To that end I have invited tour operators and travel writers to come and enjoy all that the Artemis has to offer, in the hope that they will give a glowing report. If they don't, many of those bookings could be cancelled,' Thanos added tersely. 'I hired a PR company to organise a party for the opening night. Three hundred guests have been invited, including several world-renowned celebrities. I learned yesterday that the PR company has failed to fulfil its promise that the party will be the most spectacular event ever held on Mykonos. In fact I seriously doubt they could organise a kindergarten party,' he added, his irritation palpable. 'And so this morning I fired them.'

Thanos was not a man who gave second chances, Tahlia surmised as she stared at the rigid set of his jaw, and she felt a pang of sympathy for the head of the PR company who must have borne the brunt of his fury.

'Ordinarily my PA would have alerted me to the fact that Cosmo Communications were useless,' Thanos continued. 'But Stephanie is on leave—visiting her family in South

Africa—and I have spent much of the past six months in America with Melina.'

Tahlia felt a pang of guilt for the unwitting part she had played in his sister's accident. 'What will you do? Can you find another PR consultant at such short notice?'

'I've already found one.' He leaned back in his chair and gave her a level look. 'I'm impressed by the work you did for Reynolds Gems, and I want *you* to organise the party.'

For a few seconds Tahlia was lost for words. 'That's an enormous responsibility,' she said slowly. 'Do you really trust that I can meet your expectations?'

'I trust you implicitly, Tahlia, which is why I am awarding you the contract for the Artemis party.'

The words hovered in the air between them, and for some reason Tahlia felt a lump form in her throat. 'Well, that's good to hear,' she said huskily, shocked by how much his opinion of her mattered. 'I'd be honoured to do it.' Panic kicked in as she contemplated the prestigious event he had asked her to organise at short notice. 'But how can I make arrangements for the party when I don't speak Greek?'

'A member of my staff will assist you. Ana speaks English fluently, and she can translate for you when necessary. Your job is to come up with ideas for a party that will be unforgettable and will put the Artemis on the list of the world's most exclusive hotels.'

Thanos handed her a folder.

'This is the guest list. You'll see that many of the celebrities have specific requirements on everything from the size of room they want to the colour of the towels in their bathrooms. It will be your job to ensure that they cannot find fault with the Artemis.'

Tahlia scanned through the file and noted that a well-known actress had given instructions that she was only to be served foods from those listed on her strict macrobiotic diet sheet. She would have liked six months to organise an event of this magnitude instead of three weeks, and her doubts must have shown on her face.

'I have every faith that you can do this, Tahlia,' Thanos murmured. 'And I will, of course, pay you a salary for your professional expertise,' he added in a tone that brooked no argument. 'Your work for Reynolds has proved that you have talent and a wealth of innovative ideas, which are exactly the qualities I'm looking for.'

After all the misunderstandings between them, and the contempt he had shown her when he had believed she had been his brother-in-law's mistress, the note of respect in his voice was balm to her battered self-respect. She was ashamed that she had agreed to be his mistress in return for him helping her father, but there had been no other way. Now, in offering her the party contract, she felt as though Thanos considered her an equal, and there was a new confidence in her voice when she stood up and smiled at him.

'I'd better make a start,' she said briskly. 'Three weeks will fly past.'

She refused to dwell on the knowledge that at the end of that time Thanos would no longer need her in any capacity, and that she would go home and probably never see him again. Enjoy the here and now, she bade herself as she followed him into Ana's office. She could no longer kid herself that being with him was a hardship. She was drawn to him in a way she did not understand, and she could only pray that her fascination with him would have faded by the time he ended their relationship.

'Why the frown?' Thanos queried, regarding Tahlia across the restaurant table. 'Don't you like the *baklava*?'

'Unfortunately I like it too much,' she replied ruefully, popping the last piece of the delicious pastry made with ground nuts and honey into her mouth. 'I adore Greek food— but it's not doing my waistline any good.'

'You look gorgeous to me, *agape*.' Thanos watched the flush of rosy colour stain Tahlia's cheeks and felt the same curious ache in his gut that had assailed that morning, when he had woken before her and studied her while she slept.

Three weeks in the Mediterranean sunshine had given her skin a light golden tan and added streaks of blonde to her pale red hair, making her eyes appear an even denser shade of sapphire-blue. He felt the familiar flood of heat course through his veins, but he had given up trying to fight his desire for her and instead savoured the anticipation that very soon they would return to the hotel and he would make love to her.

'So, what's troubling you?'

Tahlia gave him an incredulous look. 'The Artemis party— what else? You do realise it's a week from now? I was just thinking that I must phone the pyrotechnic company tomorrow, to check the arrangements for the firework display they're giving as a finale.'

It was one of several dozen items on her 'to do' list, she brooded anxiously. To celebrate the fact that Thanos owned hotels around the world she had decided on an international theme, and she had booked entertainers and chefs from the Caribbean, South America and the Far East to fly out to Mykonos. But, as she had feared, it was proving difficult to make the arrangements at such short notice, and her long days in the office were fraught with problems. Despite being involved in intense negotiations to buy the Ambassador Hotel in London, Thanos was taking a close interest in the party. She just hoped it would live up to his expectations.

'Ana can phone them,' Thanos told her. 'We're going to

Santorini tomorrow. I have another hotel there—the Astraea. It opened a year ago, and has already gained an excellent reputation. I thought it might be useful for you to see a hotel similar to the Artemis in operation.'

That made sense, Tahlia acknowledged. She had planned the various entertainments for the Artemis party while the hotel was empty, and she was having trouble visualising the reception rooms packed with people. 'How long do you think the trip will take? If we're going in the morning I should be able to go into the office in the afternoon.'

'Uh-uh.' Thanos shook his head, and his smile stole her breath. 'We'll be out all day—maybe all night too,' he added, a devilish gleam in his eyes. 'You've worked ten-hour days for the past two weeks and you need a break.'

He did not add that he had planned the trip so that he could spend some time alone with her away from the office, where the predominant topic of conversation between them was the forthcoming party. He could use some relaxation time too, he conceded, running his hand around the back of his neck and feeling the tight knot of tension. In the weeks after Melina's accident his usual coping strategy of suppressing his emotions had kicked in and he had functioned on auto-pilot as he'd combined running a billion-pound company with helping to nurse her. Now Melina was recovering so well that her doctors predicted she would soon be walking unaided. His relief was indescribable, but in the last six months he felt as though he had aged ten years.

He settled the bill for their meal and followed Tahlia out of the restaurant, slipping his hand into hers as they strolled along by the harbour, where fishing boats rocked gently on the calm sea. 'We're travelling to Santorini on my boat. I've a meeting scheduled with the manager of the Astraea, but it shouldn't take too long. After that we'll have the day to ourselves.'

Don't read too much into it, Tahlia told herself firmly. It was true she had worked hard these past couple of weeks. Thanos was simply being kind in offering to take her out for the day. But she could not deny her excitement at the prospect of sharing a whole day with him. Usually they only spent a few hours in the evenings together, when they ate dinner at the Artemis, or walked into Mykonos Town and found a little restaurant, before strolling back to the hotel to make love until they were both sated.

'Would you like to go to a club or head back to the Artemis?' he murmured as they passed the doors of one of the island's many nightclubs.

Would she seem too eager if she said she would prefer to return to the privacy of their suite? The gleam in his dark eyes told her he had read her mind, and she gave him an impish smile. 'I'd like to go back to the hotel.'

His brows lifted quizzically. 'You're tired?'

'Not at all.'

'Ah.' His deep laughter rumbled in his chest. 'Then an early night is definitely in order, *agape mou*. Come on—we'll walk back along the beach.'

They walked down the steps, onto the sand, and kicked off their shoes. Thanos rolled up the hems of his trousers and led her down to the shore, slipping his arm around her waist as they wandered slowly along the water's edge.

She would not be seduced by the moonlit beach, or the myriad stars that studded the velvet sky above them, Tahlia assured herself. Thanos was a charming companion, and they had enjoyed some wonderful dinners together—and of course the sex was amazing—but he meant nothing to her. But when he halted and turned her to face him she felt the familiar weakness invade her bones and knew she was kidding herself. They had become friends as well as lovers over the past weeks, and had discovered a shared interest in films and authors as well as a mutual love of travel. His dry sense of humour made her laugh, and his desire for her, which showed no sign of lessening, equalled her passion for him.

'Come back,' he murmured, his deep, gravelly voice tugging her from her thoughts. 'You keep leaving me tonight. What are you thinking about?'

About how empty my life is going to be without you, she thought silently. About how afraid I am that I'm falling in love with you.

'I was thinking about Melina,' she told him. It was not completely untrue—his sister had been on her conscience since Melina had discovered her in bed with James. She felt him stiffen, but he said nothing so she continued huskily. 'I would like to write to her and explain…that I never meant to hurt her…that I didn't know about her, and that if I had I would never have dated James. He fooled both of us,' she said sadly. 'I would do anything to change the events of that night, and I would like to tell her how sorry I am about everything.'

No sound disturbed the still air and the darkness seemed to press in on them.

'Have I made you angry?' she whispered, when she could bear his silence no longer.

'No. I'm not angry with you.' His anger was solely with himself, for the way he had misjudged her, Thanos acknowledged bleakly. He had believed the press stories about her and assumed she was a callous bitch. He had given Tahlia every reason to hate him, but during the past weeks he had come to know her, and he seriously doubted that she possessed the capacity for hatred. She had neither judged nor condemned him for the way he had treated her when he had first brought her to Mykonos, and he felt humbled by her generosity of spirit. Somehow she had slipped beneath his guard, and he wasn't sure what he was going to do about it.

'I have already explained the situation to Melina, but I think she would like to hear from you. She has moved to the convalescent wing of the hospital now. I'll give you the address.'

'Thank you.' Tahlia breathed the words against his lips as he claimed her mouth in a slow, sweet kiss that drew her urgent response. Don't fall for him, her head whispered. But her heart knew that the warning came too late.

The *Leandros* was a ninety-foot luxury yacht, so lavishly fitted out that Tahlia lapsed into stunned silence while Thanos gave her a guided tour.

'Besides the master bedroom there are four additional guest cabins, as well as staff quarters,' he told her as he led the way back through the sumptuous lounge and dining room up the stairs to the main deck. She followed him over to the seating area beneath a white canopy which billowed gently in the breeze. As she sat down a uniformed deck-hand immediately stepped forward and served them flutes of Buck's Fizz.

'It's an amazing boat,' she murmured, taking a sip of her drink and then blinking hard. 'The bubbles have gone up my nose,' she giggled self-consciously. 'I hope there's a higher ratio of orange juice than champagne. I don't usually drink alcohol at ten o'clock in the morning. It'll probably send me to sleep.'

'I will do my best to ensure you stay awake,' Thanos murmured, his eyes gleaming with amusement when she blushed.

He looked more relaxed than she had ever seen him, and utterly gorgeous in close-fitting sun-bleached jeans and a black tee shirt which was stretched tight over the powerful muscles of his chest and abdomen. His black hair was brushed back from his brow, and he looked lean and fit and so incredibly sexy that Tahlia almost melted on the spot.

His smile made her heart flip, and she grinned back at him. 'Do you take the *Leandros* out often?'

'Not as often as I'd like. Work tends to dominate my life. Melina and I used to invite a crowd of friends and cruise around the islands for a few weeks in the summer, but that stopped once she married. James's idea of fun was to go clubbing every night, and he moaned that the pace of life on the boat was too quiet,' he said grimly.

He had known from the outset that James Hamilton and Melina were not suited, he thought heavily. Given the chance, he would have done his best to dissuade his sister from marrying the brash American actor, but he'd had no opportunity to voice his doubts. Melina had arrived at his house in Athens with a cocky Hamilton in tow and revealed that they had married on the spur of the moment in Las Vegas.

'Don't be angry,' she'd pleaded, when Thanos had muttered his disapproval. 'I know James is the right man for me, and we're going to spend the rest of our lives together.'

But James had quickly grown bored with married life. He had never trusted his brother-in-law, Thanos conceded. In all honesty he had expected Melina's marriage to fail. He had known of James's reputation as a playboy, but in his fury over Melina's accident he had blamed Tahlia and refused to believe her claim that she was innocent.

At his mention of Melina and James, Thanos had fallen into a brooding silence that stretched Tahlia's nerves. 'How long will it take us to reach Santorini?' she murmured, keen to change the subject.

'We'll be there in about half an hour.' He stretched his long legs out in front of him and regarded her from behind his designer shades. 'Have you visited the Greek islands before?'

She shook her head. 'No. I backpacked around France and Spain, but other than that I've always spent my holidays with my parents in Cornwall.'

'You're close to your parents, aren't you?'

'I adore them,' Tahlia agreed. 'I'm their only child, and I guess there was a danger they could have spoiled me rotten, but they brought me up to appreciate the value of love and friendship rather than money, and they encouraged me to work hard at school so that I would have good career prospects. They would have liked more children, but Mum miscarried two babies after me and said she couldn't face the heartbreak of it happening again, so they decided to be thankful that they had one child. They're great people,' she added softly. 'I'd do anything for them—'

She broke off abruptly, wondering if Thanos would make some scathing remark about how she had sold herself to him to help her parents, but he remained silent and she quickly changed the subject again.

'Do you own hotels on any other Greek islands?'

'The Alkimini on Agistri was my first hotel, followed by the Athena on Poros, and my latest project, the Aphrodite, is currently being built on Rhodes and should be ready to open next spring. My aim is to build hotels on all the most popular islands.'

Thanos was not joking, Tahlia realised as she heard the determined note in his voice. 'How did you start your business?' she asked him curiously. 'I mean, what made you decide to build hotels?'

He was silent for a moment, considering the question, and then he said grimly, 'Desperation is probably the best answer. Desperation to keep the promise I had made my mother that I would look after Melina. I had nothing, you see. No money and little education. The only thing I had was some land on Agistri. My mother had inherited it from her family, but I did not know about it until after her death. I learned that I owned six acres of land and a spectacular view of the sea.' He laughed. 'To be honest I was not overly impressed. The ground was too rocky to farm, and its only use was as grazing land for goats. Meanwhile I was travelling to the nearby island of Aegina every day, to work as a labourer on the dozens of hotels being built there. One evening back on Agistri I watched the sun setting over the sea, and it struck me that if I could build a hotel on my land the view would be a major attraction for tourists.

'It wasn't easy,' he admitted. 'But I managed to talk the local bank manager into giving me a loan for building materials, and I convinced the island's councillors that a hotel would help Agistri's economy. For the next two years I worked on construction sites on Aegina during the day and in the evening I paid a group of labourers to help me build my hotel. The Alkimini is named after my mother. Agistri's close proximity to the mainland and Athens meant that many Greek families came for holidays, and the hotel was soon so successful that I was soon able to repay the loan and buy a prime site on the island of Poros.'

Thanos made light of his route to success, but Tahlia was sure that his life had been incredibly tough, and she felt a surge of admiration for him. 'How did you manage to take care of Melina while you were working all those hours?'

He shrugged. 'She was at school during the day, and then she would sit in the site office and do her homework. On Poros we actually lived in a Portakabin on the site while the Athena was being built, and as she grew older she often cooked for the workers. It wasn't an ideal childhood,' he said heavily. 'In the early days all the money I earned went into the business, and I often felt guilty that she missed out on the things her friends took for granted, like new clothes and school trips. But she never complained,' he said, his face softening. 'Although she did go through a stage of pestering me to get married. I think her reasoning was that if I had a wife she would no longer have to do the cooking.'

'Did you never consider it?' Tahlia murmured.

He was silent for so long that she thought he was not going to answer, but then he shrugged laconically. 'I was engaged briefly. Yalena came from my village and we grew up together. I suppose I was about fifteen when I first fell in love with her. When my parents' marriage ended, and then they both died, Yalena was the one person I could confide in. I worshipped her,' he admitted, his face hardening, 'and I believed that she loved me. I was overjoyed when she agreed to marry me. She seemed fond of Melina, and I thought we would live together as a family. But a month before our wedding Yalena admitted that she had secretly been seeing one of my closest friends.

'Takis came from one of the wealthiest families on Agistri. His father owned a fishing fleet and Takis had a secure future—whereas I had a scrubby patch of land, a crazy idea, huge debts and an orphaned kid sister.' He gave a harsh laugh. 'Hell, if I'd been in Yalena's shoes, I'd have picked the richer guy too.'

Tahlia caught the note of bitterness in his voice and her heart turned over as she imagined Thanos as a young man, struggling to make a living and care for a young child. 'What did you do when she told you?' she asked curiously.

He gave another shrug. 'What could I do? Takis was the better choice, and I loved Yalena enough that I wanted what was best for her. I released her from our engagement, gave them my blessing, and drowned my sorrows in ouzo on their wedding day,' he finished, with a self-derisive laugh that did not quite disguise the pain he had felt. At twenty he had worn his heart on his sleeve; now he was determined that no other woman would have the power to touch his emotions.

'I'm not surprised you got drunk,' Tahlia said softly. 'You had been deceived by the girl you loved, and your best friend. You must have been hurt.'

Thanos frowned. He had never spoken about his relationship with Yalena to anyone, and he did not understand why he had shared such a personal confidence with Tahlia. Maybe it was because she actually listened—unlike the self-centred women he usually dated, who only wanted to talk about themselves.

'To be honest, I had put Yalena on a pedestal,' he said grimly. 'But six months ago I discovered her true nature. She contacted me out of the blue and suggested we meet up to talk about old times. I assumed Takis would be with her, but she came to my hotel alone and made it clear that, since I was now far wealthier than her husband, she regretted dumping me all those years ago. She offered to divorce Takis, and seemed to think I would jump at the chance to marry her. She was rather put out when I turned her down,' he added sardonically. 'But I was glad I had met her again. It made me realise what a lucky escape I'd had all those years ago, and confirmed my belief that love is an illusion and marriage is an outdated institution.'

'I don't believe that,' Tahlia said quietly. 'My parents have been happily married for thirty years.'

'I guess there are always a few exceptions,' Thanos conceded. 'But my parents' marriage was destroyed by my father's infidelity, and Melina was devastated when she discovered that James was having an affair.'

Tahlia bit her lip. Thanos had told her he accepted that she had been deceived by James Hamilton, but she still felt guilty for the part she had played in ending Melina's marriage. She did not know what to say, and after a few moments she stood up and walked across the deck, leaning against the boat rail as she absorbed the beauty of the crystal-clear Aegean shimmering in the sunshine.

The *Leandros* was heading towards a land mass which rose steeply out of the sea, and as they drew nearer Tahlia saw that the reddish-brown cliffs were topped with hundreds of white houses, which from a distance looked like icing on top of a cake.

'Santorini is on the site of a volcano,' Thanos explained as he came to stand next to her. 'The cliff-sides are volcanic rock and the island forms a bay around the caldera.'

'The cliffs are so high,' Tahlia murmured, staring up at the rugged rocks towering above them.

'I believe the capital, Fira, is over two hundred metres above sea level. The views from the cable-car that you can see running up the side of the mountain are spectacular, but today we are sailing further up the coast. The Astraea is close to the village of Oia, which is reputed to have the most fantastic sunsets in the world.'

'You like your sunsets, don't you?' Tahlia teased him, remembering how he had said that watching the sun setting on Agistri had given him the idea to build a hotel there.

Thanos's mood seemed to have lightened, and he laughed. 'Sunsets and spectacular views attract tourists. We can travel up to the Astraea by car, or climb the three hundred or so steps up the cliff-side,' he told her, when the *Leandros* had sailed into the tiny port and dropped anchor.

Tahlia lifted her face to the sun and breathed in the salt tang of the sea. 'I'm game for the steps,' she assured him, her pulse racing when he caught hold of her hand. The breeze ruffled his dark hair, and his sudden grin made her heart contract.

'Okay—but don't say I didn't warn you.'

She was panting by the time they reached the top of the cliff, but her lack of breath was not only because of the steep climb, she acknowledged ruefully. Thanos kept hold of her hand as they strolled through the narrow streets of Oia, and waited patiently while she paused to admire the stunning ar-

chitecture of the blue-domed church and the jumble of sugar-
cube white houses with their window boxes full of scarlet
pelargoniums.

The Astraea was perched on the edge of the cliff, and as
Thanos had promised, offered wonderful views over the bay
and nearby islands.

'There are one or two problems that need my attention, but
I should be finished in an hour,' he told her, after he had given
her a guided tour of the hotel. 'Ask one of the reception staff
to give you directions to the beach, and I'll meet you there later.'

She had found paradise, Tahlia decided some while later,
when she had scrambled down a steep path from the hotel and
arrived at a tiny picturesque cove. The *Leandros* was moored
out in the bay, and she guessed that one of the deck hands had
brought the parasol and picnic rug, which were now arranged
on the beach, from the boat. The cove was deserted, hidden
from view by the rugged cliffs, and she stripped down to her
bikini and stretched out on the rug, wriggling her shoulders
in pleasure as the sun warmed her skin. Her eyelids felt heavy.
She hadn't had much sleep the previous night, she thought
wryly, recalling how Thanos had made love to her with all his
considerable skill, so that she had climaxed three times before
he had finally lost control and experienced his own shattering release...

'I hope you applied plenty of sunscreen.'

Thanos's deep voice roused her from a shockingly erotic
dream in which he was stroking his hands over her naked
body. She glanced at her watch and saw that she had been
asleep for almost an hour, and then let out a yelp as she felt
something cold on her back.

'You don't want to burn,' he murmured, as he began to
smooth lotion over her shoulders.

Tahlia's eyes flew open to see him lying on the rug beside her, propped up on one elbow, while he continued to smooth the cream onto her skin. He had stripped off his jeans and tee shirt and looked devastatingly sexy in a pair of navy swim-shorts, his skin gleaming like polished bronze in the sunshine. The rhythmic stroking of his hands on her back was wickedly sensuous, but she resisted the urge to turn over and pull him down on top of her.

'That should do,' she said in a strained voice, blushing furiously when she sat up and saw that her nipples had hardened and were straining beneath her Lycra bikini top. She felt his eyes slide down her body, and when she glanced at his face she was startled by the feral hunger blazing in his eyes.

'We'll spend an hour or so on the beach, and then return to the *Leandros* for a late lunch,' he said idly, brushing her hair over her shoulder and trailing his mouth up her neck.

'Good plan…' Tahlia drew a sharp breath when his teeth nipped her earlobe, sending a quiver of delicious sensation through her. 'How did your meeting go? Did you resolve the problems?'

'Concerning the Astraea, yes. But a new set of problems has arisen in the Caribbean. My hotel on St Lucia was damaged in a tropical storm that hit the island at the weekend. I'm flying out there immediately after the Artemis party.'

That meant that this time next week he would be on the other side of the world—and she would be back in England. Sudden tears blurred her vision, and she turned her head, pretending to stare at the sea while she fought to control her emotions. She had always known that their relationship was a temporary affair. The deal they had struck had been for her to spend one month with him as his mistress and soon their contract would be finished, leaving him free to continue with his own life.

Did he have a lover on St Lucia? Probably, she acknowledgedly bleakly. Ana, the Greek girl who had been helping her with the party arrangements, had said that Thanos had various mistresses around the world. A week from now he would most likely have forgotten her.

He moved his hands to her shoulders and gently tugged her towards him, but she stiffened, unable to bear the thought of making love with him while she was breaking up inside.

'I've been sunbathing for too long. I'm going to have a swim,' she choked. Tears were falling unchecked down her face, and with a muffled sob she jumped up and raced down the beach.

CHAPTER NINE

THE sea was shockingly cold on Tahlia's sun-warmed skin, but she tore through the shallows and dived beneath a wave so that her tears mingled with the spray. She struck out away from the shore, wanting to put as much distance as possible between her and Thanos, who was watching her broodingly from the beach. She swam until she was out of breath, and then flipped onto her back and allowed the waves to carry her. He was no longer sitting on the sand. She squinted against the sun, trying to spot him, and then gasped when strong arms suddenly closed around her.

'You frightened the life out of me,' she snapped, and she pushed against his chest, trying to force him to release her. But he merely tightened his grip and dragged her closer, so that she was trapped against his hard thighs. 'Let me go,' she cried frantically, hating her treacherous body as molten heat coursed through her veins, undermining her determination to resist him.

'I can't,' he growled savagely, tangling his fingers in her hair and lowering his head.

He captured her lips in a kiss of pure possession, thrusting his tongue deep into her mouth and exploring her with such erotic skill that she instantly melted. She was out of her depth in more ways than one, she acknowledged, as she tried to stand and realised that the ocean floor was far beneath her. She had no choice but to cling to Thanos for support. And as she curled her arms around his neck she knew she had lost the battle. She wanted him, *needed* him to make love to her. And when she kissed him back with feverish passion and heard the low groan torn from his throat nothing mattered except her desperation for him to possess her.

He waded back to the shallows and lowered her onto the damp sand, not lifting his mouth from hers as he came down on top of her. She was a drug in his veins, and like an addict he could not resist her lure. His hunger for her consumed him utterly, Thanos acknowledged as he stared into her eyes, as blue and crystal-clear as the Aegean.

What was it about this woman that made him wish for something more than simply sexual satisfaction? He had been a fool once before, he reminded himself savagely. Yalena had ripped his heart out, and he had sworn never to open himself up to such pain ever again. He had thought that if he made Tahlia his mistress his obsession with her would eventually fade, leaving him free to continue with a life dominated by work and occasionally enlivened by meaningless affairs with women who meant nothing to him. But as he stared down at her and saw the shimmer of tears in her eyes it struck him that he was tired of his old life.

He kissed her throat, the fragile line of her collarbone, the creamy swell of her breast. Her nipples were jutting provocatively through the wet Lycra of her bikini top, and with a muffled oath he unfastened the strings around her neck and peeled the tiny triangles down, his body tautening as he revealed her breasts in all their naked beauty.

'You are exquisite,' he said hoarsely, and he lowered his head and took first one dusky tip and then its twin into his mouth, smiling against her skin when she cried out and arched her hips in unmistakable invitation. 'I want you.' The admission was torn from him. His hands were clumsy as he dragged her bikini pants down her legs, and he struggled out of his shorts with an equal lack of finesse, his powerful erection nudging impatiently between her thighs. 'You want me too, don't you, Tahlia? We are both prisoners of the desire that thunders through our veins, and *this* is the only truth between us.'

He entered her with one savage thrust—then instantly stilled and cursed beneath his breath. 'Did I hurt you?' he demanded, his voice rasping with self-disgust at his brutality. But Tahlia's body was aroused and eagerly receptive, and she wrapped her legs around his back to prevent him from withdrawing.

'You couldn't hurt me,' she assured him softly, knowing that physically at least it was the truth. Her body had been designed for him, and she gloried in his wildfire passion that matched her own. She kissed him, telling him with her lips what she could not say out loud: that she was his for all time, and he was the keeper of her heart.

She felt him relax momentarily, but almost immediately his body was gripped with a different kind of tension as he moved, slowly at first, and then with increasing pace and strength, claiming her with a primitive hunger as he drove her higher and higher towards the climax her body craved. The sea lapped gently around them, and overhead the sun blazed in the dense blue sky. The haunting cry of a gull broke the still air, but Tahlia only was aware of Thanos's powerful body, driving into her with deep, steady strokes. She could feel his heart thudding in unison with her own, and she dug her heels into the sand, her body arching as the first spasms of exquisite pleasure ripped through her. Still he thrust, faster and faster, his breathing coming in ragged groans as he took her to the edge, kept her poised there for timeless seconds and then with one final hard stroke sent them both into freefall.

I love you. She moved her lips over his sweat-slicked chest and breathed the words she could not utter. Soon he would dismiss her from his life, and somehow she would have to live without him. It would be a colourless existence, she thought, her heart contracting painfully. The lonely days and nights ahead would seem unbearable. But he was with her now, and she clung to him as if she could somehow imprint the feel of his body on hers for all time.

'Are you all right?' he asked roughly, lifting his head from her neck and smoothing her hair back from her face with a hand that shook slightly. 'As you may have noticed, you have a disastrous effect on my self-control.' His jaw tightened, and he added in a raw tone laced with self-disgust, 'I regret that with you I become a barbarian.'

Tenderness overflowed Tahlia's heart, and she stroked her hand down his cheek. 'I don't regret your passion. I love the way you make love to me,' she whispered shyly.

He stared down at her, the expression in his dark eyes unfathomable, and she was afraid she had revealed too much. When he rolled away from her and stood up she tensed, waiting for him to make some scornful remark, but he reached his hand out to help her to her feet and drew her into his arms.

'Come to St Lucia with me?'

She must have misheard him. A gull mewed in the sky above her, and her heart hammered in her chest as she stared at him wordlessly, searching for signs that he had been joking. But the expression in his eyes was deadly serious, and her heart beat faster. Why? She wanted to ask him. For how long? A week, a month? Did it matter when her whole being was crying out to agree? she thought shakily. Nothing in life came with guarantees—losing Michael had taught her that. Why not live for the here and now, and enjoy an affair with him for however long it lasted? Was she brave enough?

'I can't,' she whispered. 'I need to go home, start looking for another job…'

'There would be no need for you to work while you are with me.'

Colour flared in her cheeks. 'I would *never* allow you to keep me. I pay my own way. It was only for my parents' sake that I…' She stumbled to a halt, shame sweeping over her at the memory of how she had sold herself to him.

'The reasons why I brought you to Mykonos are in the past,' Thanos told her fiercely. 'I want us to have a future—to enjoy our relationship for as long as either of us wants it to last.' He could not envisage a time when he would not desire her. She had captivated him like no other woman ever had. But the clichéd happy-ever-after? He'd seen too many relationships fail to contemplate commitment.

What would he say if she revealed that she wanted to be with him for ever? She stared up at his hard-boned face and acknowledged that he was as untameable as she had first thought, when she had looked across the art gallery in London and seen him. His early years had been tough, and had made him into a resolute, independent man who relied on no one, who forged his own destiny, and she doubted he would allow any woman to breach his defences.

'After St Lucia I was planning to take a break for a couple of weeks at my villa in Antigua. It's beautiful there, and we could spend some time away from everyday pressures—chill out and enjoy each other's company,' he murmured persuasively.

His mouth was a whisper away from hers, an unbearable temptation she did not have the strength to resist. 'That sounds good.' Her breath feathered his lips. 'You work too hard. Maybe I can help you to relax?'

Laugher rumbled deep in his chest. 'The last thing I feel when I am with you, *agape*, is relaxed.' His smile faded and his eyes focused intently on her face. 'You'll come?'

She ignored the feeling that she was about to cast herself off a cliff without the assurance that a safety net would catch her, and nodded. 'Yes.'

The inherent tenderness of his kiss pierced her soul, and she kissed him back with all the emotion she could not reveal in words. When he swung her into his arms she clung to his shoulders and gave him a questioning look.

'You are very lovely, *agape mou*, but also very sandy.' He grinned, looking suddenly like the boy he had been many years ago, before he had been weighed down with responsibility. 'We need to swim.' He carried her into the sea, laughing as he lowered her into the waves, and splashed her until she dived into the crystal depths. The cool water felt sensuous on her naked body, and when Thanos caught her and held her against his chest she curled her arms around his neck, her laughter fading as he captured her mouth in a hungry kiss that revealed the urgency of his need to possess her.

Thanos propped himself up on one elbow and watched the early-morning sunlight dance across Tahlia's hair, turning it into a golden halo on the pillows. Her long lashes fanned her cheeks and her face was serene. His sleeping angel, he brooded, feeling a curious tugging sensation in his chest. But the feelings she evoked in him were far from pious, and he could not resist drawing back the sheet so that the sunlight gilded her slender limbs and her small, firm breasts. Her skin felt like satin beneath his fingertips as he trailed a path over her flat stomach, then moved lower to the triangle of tight gold curls that hid her femininity. She was unutterably beautiful, and he hardened instantly as he slid his hand between her pale thighs and very gently parted her.

'Thanos?' Her lashes drifted upwards, her eyes still dazed with sleep.

'Who else were you expecting?' he demanded arrogantly.

Her smile stole his breath. 'You,' she whispered softly. 'Only you.'

She opened her mouth beneath his, welcoming the bold thrust of his tongue, and kissed him back with drowsy passion until he eased the pressure of his lips so that the kiss became a slow, sensual tasting, with an underlying tenderness that brought tears to Tahlia's eyes. Her breath hitched in her throat when he trailed his mouth down to her breast and teased her swollen nipple with his tongue, before administering the same delicious torture to its twin.

The feather-light brush of his lips on her inner thigh demolished her thought process—but something was niggling in her brain.

'Thanos! The party!'

'It's not until tonight, *agape*. I promise I'll let you up by then.'

'But there are things to do…'

She caught her breath as he lowered his head and his tongue probed delicately between her velvet folds. Moist heat pooled between her thighs and she instinctively spread her legs wider, gasping when he closed his lips around the sensitive nub of her clitoris. Sensation scorched her, and she whimpered with pleasure, desperate for him to continue his sorcery but unable to dismiss the voice in her head which pointed out that this was the day of the Artemis opening party, and she had planned to get up at dawn.

Frantically she dug her fingers into his luxuriant black hair and tugged. 'But, Thanos, I should…'

He lifted his head briefly and murmured, 'You want me to stop?'

'Yes.' She lifted her hips in mute supplication, groaning when his wickedly invasive tongue dipped between her silken folds. 'No... Don't stop—don't ever stop.'

She was trembling by the time he moved over her, and she sobbed his name as he penetrated her with deep, thrusting strokes, his movements slow and deliberate, demonstrating his complete control.

'This is all that matters, Tahlia *mou*,' he said roughly, his heart pounding so hard beneath his ribs that he felt as though he had run a marathon.

He was shocked to realise that he had spoken the truth. His need to make love to her was a driving force inside him: more important than his business, more important than the forthcoming party to celebrate the opening of his new hotel—even, he acknowledged grimly, more important than his sister. *Theos*, what was he thinking? But his powers of reasoning were slipping away, and he was conscious of nothing but the desperate clamouring of his body as he strove for the release he craved.

He slipped his hands beneath her bottom and lifted her hips, driving into her with faster and deeper strokes until she cried out. The exquisite sensation of her muscles contracting around him threatened to shatter his restraint.

'*Tahlia*.' He threw his head back, the cords on his neck straining as he fought for control. Sex had never been this good with any of his previous lovers. Only with Tahlia did he feel a sense of utter abandonment. With a harsh groan his control splintered and he shuddered, wave after wave of pleasure ripping through him until he collapsed onto her and closed his eyes, wondering why his heart ached every time he made her his.

In the aftermath he held her close, stroking his fingers

through her hair. She could stay here all day, Tahlia thought dreamily. But the Artemis party was important to him, and she wanted it to be perfect.

'Now I'll let you go to work,' he said with a grin, dropping a stinging kiss on her mouth as she gave a languorous stretch.

'Thank you, kind sir,' she teased with an impish smile before she walked unselfconsciously across the room to the *en suite* bathroom, aware of the heat in his dark eyes as he focused on her naked body.

'Have you decided what you're going to wear tonight?'

She paused in the doorway and glanced back at him, feeling the familiar dip in her stomach at the sight of his bronzed, muscular body stretched out indolently on the rumpled sheets. 'I'm not going to the party. I can't,' she continued quickly, when his brows lowered in a slashing frown. 'There will be huge media coverage tonight, and I don't want to risk being photographed with you. How would you explain my presence to Melina? It would be…awkward.' She bit her lip, rattled by his ominous silence. 'I'll ensure that all the preparations are in place, and tonight Ana will be on hand to deal with any last-minute problems.'

Thanos regarded her for a few moments, his expression unfathomable. 'Melina is my responsibility,' he said quietly. 'You don't have to worry about her. You *will* attend the party as my partner. That's an order, Tahlia,' he added forcefully, when she opened her mouth to argue. 'You've put in all the work, and tonight is your night as much as mine.' He jumped up from the bed and strode out of the room, reappearing seconds later, holding a flat box. 'I bought this for you to wear tonight.'

She gave him a startled glance, and then lifted the lid from the box and pushed aside the layers of filmy white tissue paper to reveal an ivory silk gown. With shaking fingers she took it from the box and caught her breath as she held it against her.

'Oh, Thanos…it's beautiful.' Her throat did not seem to want to work and her voice sounded distinctly rusty. The dress was exquisite: a floor-length silk sheath, covered in layers of fragile chiffon and embellished with tiny crystals and pearls on its narrow shoulder-straps and around a sweetheart neckline. 'It's a fairytale dress,' she whispered, dropping her gaze from him so that he would not see her sudden rush of tears.

He slid his hand beneath her chin and tilted her face to his. 'Tonight you will be my princess, *agape mou*.'

Her smile tugged at his insides, and the ache in his gut intensified when she reached up and brushed her lips over his in a feather-light caress that pierced him with its poignant sweetness. They needed to talk, he acknowledged as she walked into the bathroom. There were things he needed to say, to tell her. But he could not forget the original terms of the bargain they had made, and he wondered if he was a fool to hope that his money was not the only reason she gave her body to him every night with a tender passion that stirred his soul.

Tahlia was confident that all the preparations she had made over the past three weeks would ensure that the Artemis opening night party would be a success, but as she had feared there were still unexpected problems which required her attention. She spent the day making last-minute calls, organising media coverage, and attempting to meet the demands of the celebrity guests. It was early evening by the time she returned to the suite, and after a quick shower she blowdried her hair and applied minimal make-up—mascara on her lashes to emphasise the deep blue of her eyes, and a pearly pink gloss on her lips—before she stepped into the dress Thanos had chosen for her.

It was from a well-known design house and must have cost a fortune. She felt uncomfortable that he had spent so much money on her when he was already paying a huge sum for Reynolds Gems—but he had been adamant that he wanted her to wear it tonight, and she would have worn a wetsuit and flippers if it had pleased him, she acknowledged ruefully.

The door opened and he stepped into the bedroom, halting abruptly when she spun round to face him. 'You take my breath away, *agape*,' he said at length, sweeping his eyes over her in a lingering appraisal which encompassed her amber-gold hair, falling in a silky curtain around her shoulders, and the ivory dress that skimmed her slender figure.

He walked over to her and withdrew a slim velvet box from his jacket pocket. 'This will complement the dress perfectly,' he murmured, lifting out a necklace of creamy pearls inter-linked with glittering diamonds. 'It is a gift in thanks for the hours of hard work you have spent organising the party.'

'Thanos, I can't accept it,' Tahlia said faintly when he turned her to face the mirror. She stared at their twin reflec-tions: the tall, impossibly handsome man in a black dinner jacket, and the woman at his side wearing a couture gown and an exquisite necklace around her throat. 'You don't need to give me presents. I've enjoyed working at the Artemis.'

'Even so, you deserve a break. I will have to spend some time dealing with the problems at my hotel on St Lucia, but our trip to Antigua is purely for pleasure—or impurely,' he murmured wickedly, his eyes gleaming with sensual promise. 'I admit I am impatient to have you to myself, without other distractions, *agape mou*.'

His smile tugged at her heart, and when he lowered his mouth to hers, tears pricked her eyes at the sweetness of his kiss. She'd thought she had imagined the feeling of unity between them every time they made love, and had told herself she was a fool to hope that the Greek words he murmured in the aftermath of their passion meant that she was special to him.

He had once stated that love was an illusion, but the erratic thud of his heart beneath her fingertips was excitingly real.

'We need to talk,' he said quietly, when at last he broke the kiss and stared down at her flushed face. His heart turned over when her lashes swept down a fraction too late to disguise the emotion blazing in her eyes.

'But there's no time now.'

As if on cue, someone knocked on the door of the suite and his mouth tightened.

'That's probably Ana,' Tahlia said huskily. 'I'll just get my purse.'

The phone on the bedside table rang and she picked it up, frowning as the receptionist relayed a message.

'I have a call from my mother,' she told Thanos in a puzzled tone. When she had first arrived on Mykonos she had contacted her parents to explain that she was staying in Greece with a friend for a few weeks, and had given the phone number of the Artemis. An inexplicable feeling of dread coiled in her stomach. 'I hope she's okay.'

'I'll go down with Ana while you take the call,' he said, striding towards the door. 'We're not due to greet our guests for another twenty minutes.'

Tahlia watched him walk out of the room and heard him speak to Ana, followed by the snick of the door as he left the suite. 'Mum?' she gripped the phone as the sound of sobbing met her ears. 'What's wrong?'

'Oh, Tahlia, I don't understand anything,' Vivienne choked incoherently. 'Your father and I arrived back from Cornwall today to find a letter from the bank saying that Carlton House is to be repossessed. Your father admitted that he hadn't paid off the mortgage he took out to finance Reynolds Gems, and we're behind with the payments. He phoned some people— Vantage something or other…'

Vivienne paused and took a shuddering breath. 'He assured me that Vantage had agreed to buy Reynolds, and we would have the money for the house. But when he finished speaking to the CEO he was as pale as a ghost. It seems that Vantage was never interested in Reynolds. The parent company—whatever that is—refused permission for the buy-out. Dad had already assured the bank that Vantage were going to purchase Reynolds Gems, and that he would immediately clear the mortgage. But the bank checked with Vantage, and when they discovered the sale wasn't going ahead they called in the loan on Carlton.' Vivienne's voice broke. 'When your father heard that he collapsed.'

'What do you mean, he collapsed?' Tahlia demanded shakily. 'Mum…?'

'He's all right,' her mother assured her. 'Hobson called an ambulance, and the hospital did lots of checks on his heart, but all the results were fine. They say he's just suffering from extreme stress. Tahlia, I don't know what to do.'

Her mother wept, and the fear in her voice tore at Tahlia's heart.

'The bailiffs are coming at midday tomorrow to evict us, and they will seize any of our possessions that are still in the house. I don't know where to begin with the packing.' Her voice was shrill with panic. 'Our whole life is in this house.'

'Mum, you don't need to pack,' Tahlia assured her mother swiftly. 'There's been some sort of mistake. Vantage Investments definitely agreed to buy Reynolds. I'm in contact with someone at the parent company—Savakis Enterprises.' She paused and closed her eyes briefly, wondering what her mother would say if she revealed just how closely her body had been in contact with Thanos's muscular frame every night for the past month. 'Don't cry. I'll sort everything out—okay?' she said softly. 'And then I'll come home.'

It must be a mistake, she told herself frantically as she dragged out her suitcase and started to fling her belongings into it. A misunderstanding between the bank and Vantage seemed the most likely explanation. She took a deep breath, forcing herself to calm down. She would explain the situation to Thanos, and he would resolve the problem—whatever it was.

Unless *he* was the problem? a little voice whispered in her head. No, of course he wasn't. They had made a deal, and he had promised that the buy-out of Reynolds Gems would go ahead. Her relationship with Thanos was no longer based on his desire for revenge, and there was no reason why he should have reneged on his promise. She trusted him, she assured herself as she snatched up her purse, desperate to hurry down to the lobby where he was waiting for her.

But she could not dismiss the heavy sense of foreboding in the pit of her stomach, and after a moment's hesitation she turned back into the room. The likelihood that Vantage's CEO, Steven Holt, would still be in his office late on a Friday evening was remote, but if she could just speak to him first…

The phone rang several times, and she was just about to cut the call when a woman answered. 'Mr Holt is unavailable,' she said tersely. 'I'll put you through to Mark Lloyd.'

Five minutes later an impatient-sounding male voice interrupted Tahlia's frantic explanation of the reason for her call. 'Miss Reynolds, I am an executive director at Vantage Investments and I assure you I am not mistaken. It is true that we were briefly interested in buying your company, but the idea was vetoed by our parent company on the direct orders of the head of Savakis Enterprises.'

'But Mr Savakis promised me…' Tahlia insisted desperately, gripping the phone so hard that her knuckles whitened. 'You *must* be mistaken…'

'I think you'll find that it is *you* who have made a mistake,' the voice on the other end of the line said coldly. 'There is not, and never was, any deal to buy Reynolds Gems. Now, it is late, Miss Reynolds, and I would like to go home. So unless there is anything else…?'

'No…nothing else.' Tahlia's throat felt as though she had swallowed glass, and she had to force the words out. 'Thank you for clarifying the situation, Mr Lloyd.'

She replaced the receiver and sank down onto the bed. The room spun alarmingly. Surely she was not going to do something as melodramatic as faint? Bile rose in her throat and she hunched forward so that the blood rushed to her head. She couldn't faint; she had to get back to Carlton House and her parents before the bailiffs threw them onto the street.

Footsteps sounded on the marble floor, and she jerked her head round as the bedroom door opened.

'What's going on?' Thanos demanded, his eyes narrowing on her white face. 'Why haven't you come down? The guests are gathering in the lobby, waiting for the party to begin, and I want you at my side. Damn it, Tahlia,' he said explosively, when she stared at him with dull eyes. 'What's the matter with you?' He could not forget the anguished moan he'd heard as he had entered the suite. 'Are you ill?'

The pain in her heart was sheer agony—but there could still be a simple explanation for the news she had just heard, Tahlia reminded herself. Slowly she got up from the bed and faced him, her eyes locked on his face.

'Tell me, Thanos, did you ever intend to buy Reynolds Gems? Or did you bring me to Greece and make me your mistress—allow me to believe my father's problems would be solved—while all along you *knew* you had told Vantage Investments not to proceed with the buy-out?'

For a split second something indefinable flared in his eyes, before the mask fell and his expression became unfathomable.

But that tiny hesitation had told Tahlia everything—and her heart splintered.

Fool, a voice in her head taunted. Seven months ago she had believed James Hamilton when he had told her that he loved her. She had trusted him implicitly. But he had deceived her as cruelly as he had deceived his wife, and she had vowed never to give her love or trust as easily again. But here she was, with another man, in another hotel bedroom, utterly destroyed by the realisation that Thanos had lied to her. When would she learn that men either abandoned you, or lied and cheated for their own ends, and that they were not worth the heartbreak they caused? she wondered bitterly.

CHAPTER TEN

'MY MOTHER phoned to tell me that the bank has taken possession of Carlton House,' Tahlia told Thanos tensely. 'The bailiffs are due to arrive tomorrow to evict them.'

He frowned. 'Banks do not usually issue a repossession order unless there are serious mortgage arrears on a property.'

'Dad hasn't kept up with the payments on Carlton for months,' Tahlia said heavily. 'All his money has been tied up in the company. I *told* you all this,' she flung at him bitterly. 'You *knew* my parents were in danger of losing their home.'

'I had not realised that it was quite so imminent.'

'No—I suppose you thought you could string me along for a while longer before you revealed what a lying bastard you are.' Tahlia felt a curious sense of detachment as she watched his mouth tighten with anger. 'My father informed the bank that Vantage was buying Reynolds Gems, and that as soon as the sale went through he would pay off the mortgage on Carlton House. But when the bank checked with Vantage they were told that no sale had ever been agreed. Ten minutes ago I spoke to Mark Lloyd at Vantage, who verified that the buyout had been vetoed by none other than the head of Vantage Investments' parent company, Savakis Enterprises—in other words, by *you*.'

In the simmering silence following her accusation, his lack of denial felt like a knife through her heart.

Tears scalded her throat, but she forced herself to swallow them. 'You've destroyed my parents' lives, and I will *never* forgive you,' she told him, her voice shaking with emotion.

Thanos moved towards her, but halted abruptly when she flinched away from him. 'You're jumping to conclusions,' he said tersely. 'If you would give me a chance to explain—'

'In the same way that you allowed me to defend myself against your accusations that I had deliberately stolen James Hamilton from your sister, you mean?' she interrupted in a brittle voice. 'You refused to listen to me, and in your misguided quest for revenge you demanded that I became your mistress. But worst of all,' she said brokenly, tears slipping down her cheeks, 'you lied to me.'

'Listen to me,' he said urgently. 'I admit that when I first brought you to Greece I had no intention of bailing your father out of his financial mess. My sister had suffered appalling injuries, and as you know I believed you were partly responsible for her accident. The newspapers were full of reports about your wild partying, and your penchant for stealing other women's husbands, and I wanted to hurt you as I believed you had hurt Melina—' His mobile rang. With a muttered curse he answered it, and snapped impatiently, 'I'll be five minutes. Tell the bar staff to serve more champagne to the guests.'

He raked his hand through his hair and stared at Tahlia, frustration etched on his face when she glared at him. 'All that changed when I took you to bed. Sex with you was an incredible experience. I had never known such intense pleasure before,' he admitted harshly. 'And when I discovered that you were a virgin, that I had completely misjudged you…' His voice deepened with an emotion Tahlia could not define. 'I immediately phoned Steven Holt to tell him that I had changed my mind and wanted Vantage to proceed with the buy-out of Reynolds Gems.'

Tahlia recalled the phone call she'd made before Thanos had come back to the suite, and shook her head. 'I don't believe you,' she said dully. 'Mark Lloyd was adamant that Vantage have no plans to buy Reynolds Gems. One of you must be lying—and I don't think it's him.'

'You're calling me a liar?' Thanos snapped icily, his eyes darkening with anger.

His outrage, after he had refused to believe she was telling the truth about James, was almost funny—but Tahlia doubted she would ever smile again.

'I'm not sure why Mark Lloyd is involved. I left instructions with Steven Holt,' he said tersely. 'There has obviously been a misunderstanding somewhere along the line.'

Tahlia closed her suitcase and reached up to unfasten the pearl necklace that he had placed around her neck earlier. 'Mr Lloyd said that *I* had made a mistake, and he's right,' she said quietly. 'I mistakenly thought you were a man of honour, but you are a liar and a cheat, and I hope I never see you again for as long as I live.'

'*Theos*, Tahlia. You don't really mean that.' Sharp knives were ripping his insides to shreds, and he gripped her arm and swung her round to face him. 'Tell me the truth. Is the deal we made when you came to my hotel in London a month ago the only reason you have given yourself to me so passionately night after night?'

In the silence that trembled between them, Mark Lloyd's voice echoed inside Tahlia's head. *'There is not, and never was, any deal to buy Reynolds Gems.'*

How could her heart still ache for Thanos after the way he had tricked her? Tahlia wondered desperately. She must be the biggest fool on the planet. But at least she retained sufficient pride to hide her stupidity from him.

'What other reason could there have been?' she demanded coolly. 'I believed you were paying me to be your mistress.'

His eyes were so hard and cold that she took a hasty step backwards.

'I must congratulate you on your exemplary performance every night,' he said, in a dangerously soft voice that sent a trickle of ice down her spine. 'Perhaps you should consider whoring as a new career.'

She closed her eyes briefly as pain tore through her. 'I have to go,' she muttered, grabbing her case and heading for the door. 'I need to get back to my parents.'

Thanos strolled towards her, reminding her of a sleek, dark panther stalking its prey. 'Aren't you forgetting something?'

'I put the necklace on the bedside table. You saw me.'

He smiled pleasantly, like a wolf before it sprang for the kill. 'Not the necklace—the dress.'

'Oh.' She shook her head, feeling an idiot. The old skirt and top she'd left out to travel in—*her* clothes, not the ones he had bought her—were on the bed. 'I'll get changed in the bathroom.'

'I'd like it back *now*.'

The gleam in his eyes warned her that he would have no compunction in stripping the dress from her body. She was breaking up inside, but she would not let him see it. 'What is this, Thanos? Last-minute titillation?' she demanded scornfully, and she reached behind her and slid the zip down her spine. He must have known the dress did not require her to wear a bra, but she refused to drop her gaze from his as she allowed the silk gown to slither to the floor.

Dull colour scorched his cheekbones. 'We both know I could take you right now and you would do nothing to stop me,' he said roughly.

There was little point in denying it when her nipples were

jutting eagerly towards him, begging for the tender ministrations of his hands and mouth. But she tore her eyes from him and managed a nonchalant shrug. 'So you press all the right buttons. You're a fantastic stud, Thanos.'

She swung away from him and clumsily dragged on her skirt and tee shirt, hating the way her breasts were tingling in anticipation. She would *never* allow him to touch her again, would *never* make love with him again and know the indescribable pleasure that she had only ever experienced with him. Her eyes ached with tears as she stumbled to the door, but there was one last thing she needed to know.

'How long had you anticipated our relationship lasting after the trip to Antigua?'

Thanos stared at the streaks of tears and mascara running down her face and felt an overwhelming urge to pull her into his arms and kiss her, until she acknowledged that what they had shared this past month was too good to throw away. But obviously she did not think so, he brooded bitterly. She had come to him in London because she'd needed his money to help her father, and no doubt she had agreed to go to the Caribbean with him because she enjoyed the benefits associated with being the mistress of a millionaire. She was no better than Yalena, and the countless other women who saw dollar signs when they looked at him. He was better off without her.

'I hadn't planned on it lasting at all. I'm not a fan of commitment,' he drawled sardonically. 'A few weeks of sun, sea and sex are all I have ever wanted from any woman, and you are no different.'

'I see.' The tiny flame of hope inside her died, but she could not drag her eyes from him as she committed to memory his sculpted features and his hard body sheathed in the superbly cut black dinner suit—before she turned and walked out of his life.

* * *

By the time Tahlia reached the airport she had missed the last plane to London, but she was so desperate to leave Mykonos that she caught the next flight to Athens and, after spending a sleepless night in the terminal there, managed to book a seat on the first flight to Gatwick the following morning. As the taxi turned through the gates of Carlton House she half expected to see the bailiffs waiting on the drive, but to her relief there was just her father's car parked by the front steps.

'They're not here yet, then?' she murmured, when her mother opened the door and immediately burst into tears at the sight of her. 'Where's Hobson?'

'Unpacking,' Vivienne mumbled, wiping her eyes.

'Unpacking? But…I thought you had to be ready to leave by midday?'

'No.' Vivienne shook her head, looking as dazed as Tahlia felt. 'We can stay. Apparently the money for Reynolds Gems was paid into our bank account late last night, and first thing this morning your father cleared the mortgage. I don't pretend to understand what's going on, but Dad says that everything has been sorted out. Isn't it wonderful, darling?' She gave Tahlia a watery smile. 'The last twenty-four hours have been a rollercoaster.'

'It's brilliant news,' Tahlia said slowly.

Why had Thanos done it? she wondered. Had she damaged his pride when she had proved him to be a liar? She longed to send the money straight back to him, but Carlton House was saved, and her mother was smiling again, and that was really all that mattered, she told herself wearily.

'How's Dad?'

'Relieved—as you can imagine—and resting. He's admitted he hasn't slept properly for months.' Vivienne sighed. 'I wish he had told me about our financial problems rather than going through all that worry on his own.'

'He was trying to protect you,' Tahlia said softly. Her parents' love for each other was as strong as it had been on the day they had married. Some marriages lasted. But Thanos thought that marriage was an outdated institution, and she could not believe she had been so stupid as to hope that he might have begun to care for her a little.

'I have another piece of news,' her mother said gently. 'Aunt George passed away in her sleep two days ago. She was ninety-two, you know. Dear Georgie—she told everyone she was five years younger.'

Charlie stalked into the room, his tail held high, and sprang onto Tahlia's lap, purring loudly when she buried her face in his ginger fur.

Vivienne patted her shoulder and reached for the box of tissues. 'I'm sorry, darling. I know how fond of her you were,' she murmured, unaware that Tahlia's tears were not just for her aunt, but for an enigmatic Greek man who had stolen her heart.

A week later, Tahlia stared at the cheque on the desk in front of her. Then she lifted her gaze to the family's elderly solicitor, Harold Wimbourne, her eyes wide with shock. 'I had no idea Aunt George was so wealthy,' she said faintly.

'Miss Prentice was a shrewd investor on the stockmarket,' the solicitor explained. He cleared his throat and added conspiratorially, 'I believe she also made a fortune from betting on the horses. Your aunt bequeathed to you her flat in Pimlico, and various other assets detailed in her will. She also set up a trust fund which was to mature on your twenty-fifth birthday or on her death—whichever happened first. As trustee of the fund, I have the happy task of handing you that cheque.' He chuckled. 'I can see it has come as a bit of a shock. I don't suppose you have any idea yet about what you'd like to do with the money?'

'A bit of a shock' was an understatement, Tahlia thought numbly as the row of noughts swam in front of her. She gave Harold a faint smile and said steadily, 'Actually, I know exactly what I'm going to do with it. I assume I can spend it straight away?'

'Oh, yes. It's yours to spend in whichever way you choose, my dear. I can advise you on secure investments, and so on, but I'm sure Georgina wanted you to have fun with it.'

Tahlia could not imagine a time when she would ever have fun again, but she was grateful to her aunt for giving her the means to restore a little of her pride. Immediately she sent Thanos a cheque for half the amount he had paid for Reynolds Gems, and an assurance that she would send him the remainder once she had sold the flat.

You paid for my body and treated me as your whore, but now I am buying back my self-respect, she scribbled furiously. *I wonder if you will ever be able to regain yours, Thanos?*

But he had not really treated her like a whore, she acknowledged honestly, as the week dragged into the next and the pain of missing him grew worse with every day. He'd accepted that she had not known James Hamilton was married to his sister, and, with his reason for wanting revenge no longer valid, it did not make sense that he had double-crossed her—especially as the day after she had walked out on him he had paid her father for Reynolds Gems.

Doubt gnawed at her as she recalled his insistence that he *had* instructed the CEO of Vantage Investments to buy Reynolds. Maybe she had been too hasty when she'd refused to listen to him? But she had been so afraid that he had deceived her, as James had done, and so unbearably hurt at the idea that he had tricked her. And then he had revealed that he had only invited her to his villa in Antigua to be his convenient sex partner. She had been kidding herself that their relationship might develop into something deeper, she acknowledged miserably. She'd known of his reputation as a commitment-phobic playboy, and it was her own fault that her heart was shattered beyond repair.

Thanos watched the rain bounce off the windscreen, and wondered how much longer he would have to sit outside Tahlia's flat waiting for her to return. He would sit here for the rest of his life if necessary, he thought grimly, but when he glanced at his watch and saw that barely five minutes had crawled past since he had last checked his frustration escalated.

He had received her cheque a week ago, and since then it had been burning a hole in his pocket—along with her terse note questioning whether he would ever be able to regain his self-respect. Anger surged through him, but he fought to control it. He had been angry on the night of the Artemis party, when she had accused him of tricking her about buying Reynolds Gems. Fury had burned in his gut that she did not trust him. But later, when his temper had cooled, he'd conceded that he had done little to earn her trust. He had believed every damnable lie the tabloid press had written about her, and forced her to become his mistress without giving her a chance to defend herself. His treatment of her had been unforgivable, he thought wearily. He was probably wasting his time sitting here, but he had discovered over the past two weeks that, as he could neither work nor sleep, he had a lot of time to waste.

A figure came into view, head bowed against the rain, the pale red hair instantly recognizable. The dejected slump of her shoulders tugged at Thanos's insides. She'd lost weight, he noted, his mouth tightening. She looked achingly fragile, and even more beautiful than the woman who had haunted him night and day for the past two weeks. He longed to snatch her into his arms and simply hold her, but as his eyes lingered on her breasts, clearly outlined beneath her damp top, he acknowledged that holding her would not be enough. His body stirred, but he ruthlessly ignored the sharp clamour of desire. There were things he must say, and this time he was determined she would listen to him.

Tahlia dumped the bag of groceries on the kitchen table and pushed her wet hair impatiently out of her eyes as she unpacked a week's worth of cat food. 'At least one of us still has an appetite,' she muttered, when Charlie wound around her ankles.

The doorbell pealed and she groaned, tempted to ignore it. Although she had not confided the full details of her relationship with Thanos to her friends, they had guessed that she was suffering from 'man trouble' and were running a campaign to drag her out of the depression that some days seemed to swamp her. She knew they meant well, but she seriously doubted she would ever get over him, and she preferred to be on her own.

The bell rang again and, cursing beneath her breath, she walked down the hall and opened the door.

'Hello, Tahlia.'

The gravelly, accented voice was so poignantly evocative that tears stung her eyes. She had experienced the same peculiar rushing noise in her ears on the night she had discovered his deception, but this time she could not control the feeling that she was on a carousel, spinning faster and faster. It was a relief when blackness claimed her.

She opened her eyes to find herself lying on the sofa, Thanos's furious face inches from hers as he crouched beside her. '*Theos*, why haven't you been eating?' he demanded roughly.

'I do eat,' she lied, forcing herself to sit up, relieved that the walls were no longer revolving.

'You're too thin,' he insisted harshly, 'and too pale; there are shadows beneath your eyes.

'So? I haven't been sleeping too well.' She would rather die than have him guess that she was pining away for him. 'I've been having bad dreams,' she told him pointedly, tilting her chin. 'Why are you here, Thanos?'

He stood up, but to her dismay settled himself next to her on the sofa—so close that she was conscious of his hard thigh muscle pressing against her jeans. 'Firstly, I want an answer,' he said coolly. 'Are you pregnant? I did not use protection when I made love to you on the beach on Santorini,' he said, when she gave him a startled look.

She made her decision in a split second. 'No,' she said quickly, praying he had not heard the faint tremor in her voice.

When he made no reply she risked another glance, but his face was expressionless. 'I see,' he murmured at last. 'Then that leads us to the second reason for my visit—which is to return this.' He withdrew the cheque she had sent him from his jacket pocket and held it out to her.

'Keep it,' she said sharply. 'I know you transferred the money for Reynolds Gems into my father's account the day after I left Mykonos, but now I'm repaying every penny. My family are no longer indebted to you.'

He tore the cheque into pieces with tightly leashed savagery and said harshly, 'When I first met you I believed you had seduced my sister's husband as callously as my father's mistress had wrecked my parents' marriage. I could see little to differentiate you from Wendy, and I transferred the hatred I had felt for her onto you.'

She almost preferred his lies to his brutal honesty, Tahlia thought numbly.

A tremor of sheer misery ran through her, causing Thanos to frown. 'You should change out of your wet clothes,' he said

abruptly. When she shook her head he gave an impatient sigh
and shrugged out of his jacket, draping it around her shoulders. The leather collar was as soft as butter against her cheek,
and the silk lining carried the lingering scent of his cologne.
His compassion, when seconds before he had been compar-
ing her to his father's mistress, twisted the knife in Tahlia's
heart. She wished he would just say what he had come to say
and leave—before she broke down in front of him.

'While we were on Mykonos I was heavily involved with
the negotiations to buy the Ambassador Hotel in London,' he
said quietly. 'And of course the Artemis party was looming.
Vantage Investments *is* a subsidiary company of Savakis
Enterprises, but it functions as an independent company. After
I had instructed Steven Holt to proceed with buying Reynolds
Gems I had no reason to contact him again. I was unaware
until the night you left Mykonos that Steven's wife had gone
into premature labour the day after I had spoken to him. Their
son was born twelve weeks early, and Steven has barely left
the hospital since the birth. I understand that the baby is still
in the special care unit, but he is now thriving,' he murmured,
when Tahlia looked horrified.

'Perhaps understandably, Steven forgot to pass on the
message to Mark Lloyd about my change of decision over the
purchase of Reynolds Gems. Once I discovered what had
happened I immediately transferred money from my personal
account to your father's bank.'

Without Thanos's swift intervention her parents would
have lost their home, Tahlia acknowledged, guilt sweeping
through her when she recalled how she had accused him of
being a liar.

He stood up and walked over to the window, staring at the
rain lashing against the glass. 'If I am honest, I knew almost
from the start that you were nothing like Wendy—or the

vacuous bimbo portrayed by certain tabloids,' Thanos continued tensely. 'You were gentle and kind.' He glanced dispar-
agingly at Charlie, who was curled up in an armchair like a
fluffy ginger cushion. 'You rescued stray animals. I wanted
to hate you,' he said roughly, 'but you got under my skin and
I discovered that I enjoyed being with you. I wanted to come
after you the night you left, but I couldn't leave Ana to cope
alone at the party—and I was furious that, although the month
that we had been lovers had been the happiest of my life, you
clearly did not feel the same way. You did not trust me. The
next morning I learned that the damage to my hotel on St
Lucia was more serious than I had first realised, and that
several of my staff had been injured in the storm. I had no
choice but to fly immediately to the Caribbean.'

Tahlia could think of nothing to say as she absorbed his
words, and a tense silence quivered between them before
Thanos finally spoke again.

'I'm sorry for the way I treated you when we first met. I
blamed you for hurting my sister, and in my damnable desire
for revenge I stole your innocence.'

The bleakness in his eyes tore at Tahlia's heart, and even
in the midst of her misery she wanted to absolve him. 'Neither
of us could deny the sexual chemistry between us,' she said
softly. 'I wanted you to make love to me.'

She got to her feet and held out his jacket, praying he
would take the hint and go, but he strode towards her, his eyes
blazing, and threw the jacket carelessly onto the sofa.

'I dishonoured you,' he said harshly. 'And the only way I
can try to make amends is to marry you.'

'What?' Tahlia's jaw dropped, and as the room tilted alarmingly she was afraid she was going to faint again.

Thanos was deadly serious, she realised as she stared at his
taut face, his skin stretched tightly over the razor-sharp edges

of his cheekbones. He was impossibly beautiful, and equally impossible to understand—although in a way she did understand his reasoning. At heart he was a traditional Greek male and an honourable man. His self-respect had been badly damaged by what he perceived as the wrong he had done to her. But *marriage*! That was taking contrition a step too far.

'I don't want to marry you,' she said quietly.

Thanos felt as though he had received a hammer-blow to his heart. It was the same pain he had experienced when Yalena had broken their engagement and revealed that she had been sleeping with Takis; the same pain that had ripped through him when he had seen Melina for the first time after the accident, when she had looked so tiny amid all the wires and tubes which had been keeping her alive.

'You must know I would never do anything to hurt you,' he said roughly. 'And I am a wealthy man—you would not want for anything.'

Dear heaven, this was torture. Didn't he realise that her resolve was perilously close to crumbling? That she longed to snatch this chance of happiness even though she knew she would never be truly happy when he did not love her?

'But I would want something that you cannot give me, Thanos,' she whispered, forcing the words past the constriction in her throat. 'I would want love. I don't care about your wealth or the material things you can give me. I would marry you if you were a goat-herd on Agistri if you loved me as much I love you.'

Tears blurred her vision, so she felt rather than saw him move, but she guessed that her admission would have him striding out of the door without a backward glance. She was unprepared for the strong arms that closed around her, and she gave a startled cry when the walls revolved again as he lifted her and carried her down the hall.

'Thanos, what are you doing?' she choked, unable to stem the tears that had been gathering since he had first appeared on her doorstep.

He kicked open her bedroom door and lowered her gently onto the bed. Her heart turned over when she saw that his thick eyelashes were spiked with moisture.

'Thanos?' She raised a trembling hand to his cheek, her eyes widening at the unguarded expression in his eyes as he knelt over her.

'You love me?' he said in a strained tone, all his arrogance stripped away, leaving him achingly vulnerable.

It was small wonder that he sounded disbelieving, Tahlia thought gently. Years ago he had been so cruelly rejected by the woman he had loved. Since then he had shouldered the responsibility of bringing up his sister and building a hugely successful company, and she guessed that deep down he had never come to terms with being abandoned by his both his parents. For most of his life he had felt alone.

Her pride suddenly seemed unimportant—especially when he was staring at her as if her answer mattered desperately to him. 'I love you with all my heart,' she assured him quietly.

He closed his eyes briefly and drew a ragged breath. 'You are my world, Tahlia *mou*,' he said simply, his voice shaking with emotion. 'And I will love you and cherish you until I die. You stole my heart, and now it is yours for ever.' He kissed away the tears slipping down her face. 'Does knowing that I love you make you cry?' he murmured, and the shadow of uncertainty in his eyes tugged at her heart.

'Only because I have wanted you to love me for so long and I can't believe it has happened,' she said shakily.

'Believe it,' he bade her urgently, taking her hand and holding it over his heart, so she could feel its thunderous beat pass through her fingertips into her veins. 'The month we spent together on Mykonos was the happiest I have ever known, and day by day my feelings for you grew more intense. Now you know that I love you with my heart and soul and everything I am, will you do me the honour of marrying me, *agape mou*?'

She saw the love that blazed in his eyes, and finally began to hope that everything really would be all right.

'Melina…?' she queried anxiously.

'Melina knows how I feel about you and she gives us her blessing. In fact, she says if you don't agree to be my wife she'll catch the next plane to England and try to persuade you herself,' he quipped lightly, his smile not disguising the fierce tension that still gripped him. 'She's looking forward to meeting you and getting to know you properly.'

That left one last doubt, Tahlia acknowledged, catching her lower lip with her teeth. 'I love you, and I would love to marry you.' She pressed her finger to his mouth when he bent his head to kiss her. 'But I have a confession. I lied to you, Thanos.' He held her gaze steadily, and she took a deep breath. 'When you asked if I was pregnant I denied it. I didn't want you to come back to me out of duty.'

She suddenly felt ridiculously shy, and the look of dawning comprehension in his eyes gave no clue to how he felt.

'*Tahlia?*'

'I going to have your baby,' she said softly. 'Are you…are you pleased?' She watched his smile widen to a grin that made him look almost boyish, and her heart overflowed with her love for him.

'*Pleased* is such an inadequate word to express how I feel, *agape*,' he said deeply, his voice cracking with the emotion. 'Overjoyed is better—and thankful, humbled that I have found you, *pedhaki mou*. And most of all determined that you will never have reason to doubt my love for you and our child.'

He bent his head again and claimed her mouth in a kiss that spoke of passion and desire and a powerful, abiding love that would last a lifetime.

Tahlia responded to him with everything that was in her heart, so that the kiss became a sensual feast that fanned the flames of their mutual hunger. Their clothes were a barrier he swiftly removed, and she cried his name as he cupped her breasts and teased each rosy tip with his tongue. He groaned when she traced her fingers over his body, and fought for control when she encircled him and caressed him until he could not wait a second longer.

'I love you,' he whispered as he gently parted her and discovered the drenching sweetness of her arousal.

She was the love of his life, and he told her so as he entered her and joined their bodies as one, moving with exquisite care until passion overwhelmed them both and they reached the heights together before tumbling back to earth to lie replete in each other's arms, their hearts beating in unison.

EPILOGUE

THEY were married six weeks later, in the village church where Tahlia had been christened, and they held a reception for family and friends in a huge marquee on the lawn at Carlton House.

Melina was well enough to fly over from America, accompanied by a tall, handsome doctor. She revealed that Daniel Sanders had asked her to marry him.

'We've both fallen in love with the right man this time,' she murmured to Tahlia as the guests gathered on the driveway to watch the bride and groom depart for their honeymoon in Antigua.

Tahlia had felt nervous about meeting Thanos's sister, but Melina had quickly assured her that she did not blame anyone but her ex-husband for the collapse of her marriage.

'Do you think Thanos approves of Daniel?' Melina asked anxiously, as Tahlia was about to climb into the limousine next to her new husband.

'He likes him very much,' Tahlia reassured her. 'But I can't believe you want me to be your bridesmaid. My obstetrician has already said that the baby is bigger than average. I'm going to look like a whale in six months' time.'

'What was your whispered conversation with Melina about?' Thanos murmured when the car finally sped away.

Tahlia gave her parents one last wave and turned back to smile at him. 'She wanted to know if you approve of Daniel—I told her that you did.'

'I think he'll make her happy.' Thanos lifted Tahlia's hand to his mouth and pressed his lips to the plain gold wedding band that he had slipped onto her finger, next to her diamond solitaire engagement ring, during the ceremony. 'And I will spend the rest of my life making *you* happy, Tahlia *mou*,' he told her seriously. '*S'agapo*. I love you.'

The raw emotion evident in his dark eyes brought a lump to her throat, and her mouth trembled slightly as she kissed him. 'And I love you. Always and for ever.'

They spent a blissful month in Antigua, before returning to Thanos's stunning villa in a leafy suburb of Athens. Tahlia's parents were frequent visitors, and Thanos refused to be away from home for more than one night, ruthlessly delegating business trips to his executives.

By the end of her pregnancy Tahlia was as big as she had predicted. 'You don't look like a whale. You are my beautiful and very pregnant wife,' Thanos told her softly when she bemoaned her expanding waistline, 'and I love you more than words can say.'

He said those words over and over when she went into labour a week early, and said them again in a voice choked with emotion when she gave birth to their son. They called him Petros. And as Tahlia held her newborn son to her breast, and stroked his shock of dark hair, Thanos claimed her mouth in a lingering kiss.

'You are never going through that again,' he muttered rawly, unable to forget the sight of her pain-ravaged face as she delivered their baby. 'I would have given everything I own if I could have suffered in your place.'

'It wasn't so bad,' Tahlia assured him, her labour pains

already forgotten as she stared in wonder at the precious new life in her arms. 'I always wanted a brother or sister when I was growing up, and I don't want Petros to be an only child. Three children is a nice-sized family, don't you think?'

Thanos stroked a lock of damp hair from her face, and closed his eyes briefly as emotion swept through him. 'I think you are incredible, *kardia mou*, and there are not the words to say how much I love you. You know I'd agree to half a dozen children if it's what you want. But for now we have Petros, and we share a love that will last a lifetime. I could not ask for more, my love, because you are everything.'

* * * * *

*Harlequin Presents® is thrilled to
introduce a sexy new duet,*
HOT BED OF SCANDAL, *by Kelly Hunter!*
Read on for a sneak peek of the first book
EXPOSED: MISBEHAVING WITH THE MAGNATE.

'I'M ATTRACTED to you and don't see why I should deny it. Our kiss in the garden suggests you're not exactly indifferent to me. The solution seems fairly straightforward.'

'You want me to become the comte's convenient mistress?'

'I'm not a comte,' Luc said. 'All I have is the castle.'

'All right, the billionaire's preferred plaything, then.'

'I'm not a billionaire, either. Yet.' His lazy smile warned her it was on his to-do list. 'No, I want you to become my outrageously beautiful, independently wealthy lover.'

'Isn't that the same option?'

'No, you might have noticed that the wording's a little different.'

'They're just words, Luc. The outcome's the same.'

'It's an attitude thing.' He looked at her, his smile crookedly charming. 'So what do you say?'

To an affair with the likes of Luc Duvalier? 'I say it's dangerous. For both of us.'

Luc's eyes gleamed. 'There is that.'

'Not to mention insane.'

'Quite possibly. Was that a yes?'

Gabrielle really didn't know what to say. 'So how do we start this thing? If I were to agree to it. Which I haven't.' Yet.

'We start with dinner. Tonight. No expectations beyond a pleasant evening with fine food, fine wine and good company. And we see what happens.'

'I don't know,' she said, reaching for her coffee. 'It seems a little…'

'Straightforward?' he suggested. 'Civilized?'

'For us, yes,' she murmured. 'Where would we eat? Somewhere public or in private?'

'Somewhere public,' he said firmly. 'The restaurant I'm thinking of is a fine one—excellent food, small premises and always busy. A man might take his lover there if he was trying to keep his hands off her.'

'Would I meet you there?' she said.

'I will, of course, collect you,' he said, playing the autocrat and playing it well. 'Shall I meet you there,' he murmured in disbelief. 'What kind of question is that?'

'Says the new generation Frenchman,' she countered. 'Liberated, egalitarian, nonsexist…'

'Helpful, attentive, chivalrous…' he added with a reckless smile. 'And very beddable.'

He was that.

'All right,' she said. 'I'll give you the day—and tonight—to prove that a civilized, pleasurable and manageable affair wouldn't be beyond us. If you can prove this to my satisfaction, I'll make love with you. If this gets out of hand, however…'

'Yes?' he said silkily. 'What do you suggest?'

Gabrielle leaned forward, elbows on the table. Luc leaned forward, too. 'Well, I don't know about you,' she murmured, 'but I'm a clever, outrageously beautiful, independently wealthy woman. I plan to run.'

This sparky story is full of passion, wit and scandal and will leave you wanting more!
Look for
EXPOSED: MISBEHAVING WITH THE MAGNATE
Available March 2010

*Two families torn apart by secrets and desire
are about to be reunited in*

a sexy new duet by

Kelly Hunter

EXPOSED: MISBEHAVING WITH THE MAGNATE

#2905 Available March 2010

Gabriella Alexander returns to the French vineyard she
was banished from after being caught in flagrante with the
owner's son Lucien Duvalier–only to finish what they started!

REVEALED: A PRINCE AND A PREGNANCY

#2913 Available April 2010

Simone Duvalier wants Rafael Alexander and always has, but
they both get more than they bargained for when a night of
passion and a royal revelation rock their world!

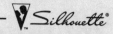

SPECIAL EDITION

FROM *USA TODAY* BESTSELLING AUTHOR
CHRISTINE RIMMER

A BRIDE FOR JERICHO BRAVO

Marnie Jones had long ago buried her wild-child
impulses and opted to be "safe," romantically
speaking. But one look at born rebel Jericho Bravo
and she began to wonder if her thrill-seeking side
was about to be revived. Because if ever there was
a man worth taking a chance on, there he was,
right within her grasp....

*Available in March
wherever books are sold.*

Visit Silhouette Books at www.eHarlequin.com

SSE65511

LARGER-PRINT BOOKS!

HARLEQUIN *Presents*

PASSION GUARANTEED SEDUCTION

GET 2 FREE LARGER-PRINT NOVELS PLUS 2 FREE GIFTS!

YES! Please send me 2 FREE LARGER-PRINT Harlequin Presents® novels and my 2 FREE gifts (gifts are worth about $10). After receiving them, if I don't wish to receive any more books, I can return the shipping statement marked "cancel". If I don't cancel, I will receive 6 brand-new novels every month and be billed just $4.55 per book in the U.S. or $5.24 per book in Canada. That's a saving of 13% off the cover price! It's quite a bargain! Shipping and handling is just 50¢ per book in the U.S. and 75¢ per book in Canada.* I understand that accepting the 2 free books and gifts places me under no obligation to buy anything. I can always return a shipment and cancel at any time. Even if I never buy another book, the two free books and gifts are mine to keep forever.

176 HDN E4GC   376 HDN E4GN

Name _____ (PLEASE PRINT)

Address _____ Apt. #

City _____ State/Prov. _____ Zip/Postal Code

Signature (if under 18, a parent or guardian must sign)

Mail to the **Harlequin Reader Service:**
IN U.S.A.: P.O. Box 1867, Buffalo, NY 14240-1867
IN CANADA: P.O. Box 609, Fort Erie, Ontario L2A 5X3

Not valid for current subscribers to Harlequin Presents Larger-Print books.

**Are you a subscriber to Harlequin Presents books
and want to receive the larger-print edition?
Call 1-800-873-8635 today!**

* Terms and prices subject to change without notice. Prices do not include applicable taxes. Sales tax applicable in N.Y. Canadian residents will be charged applicable provincial taxes and GST. Offer not valid in Quebec. This offer is limited to one order per household. All orders subject to approval. Credit or debit balances in a customer's account(s) may be offset by any other outstanding balance owed by or to the customer. Please allow 4 to 6 weeks for delivery. Offer available while quantities last.

Your Privacy: Harlequin Books is committed to protecting your privacy. Our Privacy Policy is available online at www.eHarlequin.com or upon request from the Reader Service. From time to time we make our lists of customers available to reputable third parties who may have a product or service of interest to you. If you would prefer we not share your name and address, please check here. ☐

Help us get it right—We strive for accurate, respectful and relevant communications. To clarify or modify your communication preferences, visit us at www.ReaderService.com/consumerchoice.

HPLP10